Ghostly Business

Lorna Shadow cozy ghost mystery - book 5

K.E. O'Connor

K.E. O'Connor Books

GHOSTLY BUSINESS
Copyright © 2023 by K.E. O'Connor
ISBN: 978-1-915378-61-3
Written by: K.E. O'Connor

Chapter 1

"If we take out this old fireplace, the room will be much bigger. This could be a great sized living room." Zach Booth tapped his knuckles on the top of the crumbling fire surround.

"I sort of like that fire. It adds character." I did a slow pivot as I looked around the room of the house we were considering buying.

All the rooms had lovely high ceilings and a spacious feel. And the place was empty, so we'd be able to buy quickly. I should have adored it, but I couldn't shake off the sensation I was being watched.

"We can keep the fireplace." Zach walked over and wrapped his arms around me, resting his stubbled chin on my shoulder. "What do you think of the place? Do you get a good feel?"

I gave a shrug, not wanting to let him down when he'd worked so hard to get us through the door of the house as soon as it came on the market. "Like we might be spied upon in bed."

When Zach asked me about the *feel* of a place, he wasn't talking about the vibes of the house. He wanted to know if any ghosts were living there.

My ability to see ghosts had been a sticking point in our relationship, but Zach was slowly coming around to the fact that if he loved me, he had to at least tolerate the ghosts. We'd decided to buy a house together, but only one that had no resident ghosts.

Finding that perfect house was proving trickier than I'd thought it would be. We were on our twentieth house viewing, and every time I'd viewed a property, I'd seen a ghost. It sometimes felt like they were stalking me.

"There are plenty of other places we can view," Zach said. "I only suggested this one because the location is so good."

"It's a great location, nice and central." I leaned back against Zach, relaxing in his embrace and enjoying the feel of his strong arms holding me tightly.

This was a good step in our relationship, but it would be the first time I'd ever shared a house with a boyfriend. I had to admit, I was nervous about the move, but it was coupled with excitement. If only we could find a place we loved that didn't come with any ghostly sitting tenants.

"Let's check out the dining room." Zach took my hand, his calloused palm feeling warm and solid. As a gardener, Zach would always be a little rough around the edges, but I liked him that way.

We walked out of the empty living room and across the hallway, into the dining room. There was no furniture in this room, but the large bay window let in plenty of light, and dust motes danced around in the autumn sunshine as I checked out the space.

Flipper and Jessie bounded into the room, chasing each other in play. Flipper turned toward Jessie and ducked, before bouncing up and out of her reach.

Jessie's dark eyes sparkled and her black fur gleamed in the sunshine as she gave a bark of pleasure before chasing after Flipper.

"Those two have given it their seal of approval." Zach grinned as he watched the dogs playing.

"They'll live anywhere, so long as they have each other." I turned and ran a hand down Zach's face. "Same goes for me. I don't mind where we live, just so long as we're together."

"So, if I suggest a tent in the middle of Dartmoor, you'd be happy with that?" Zach smiled as he tucked a strand of my dark bob behind my ear.

I snitched my nose at him. "You're pushing this relationship too far by suggesting a tent. And we're not the only ones we need to consider."

"The dogs won't mind a tent." Zach's grin widened.

I jumped at the sound of stamping footsteps over our heads, and sighed. "You know I wasn't talking about them."

My best friend, Helen Holiday, was stomping around upstairs, her voice high and angry.

I knew the reason for her frustration. It came in a tall dark package. And this particular package had confidence oozing from his pores, and never let Helen get one over on him. Gunner Booth, Zach's brother, delighted in teasing her whenever he got the chance. And he'd be doing it all the more when we finally found a place we could all agree on.

"You don't need the room with the attached bathroom. Look at the state of you, you can't spend more than two minutes a day in the bathroom." Helen's voice grew closer as her feet pounded down the stairs, closely followed by another set.

"We can share the room if you like it so much," Gunner said.

So far, the four of us hadn't been able to agree on where we wanted to live and what we wanted to buy. I kept seeing ghosts; Helen complained that the bedrooms were too small and she needed an attached bathroom; Zach wanted outside space so he could hone his already amazing horticultural skills, and Gunner, well, he was easy. He just needed a place to rest his head and plenty of food in the refrigerator.

Helen charged into the dining room, bright pink spots of color on her heart-shaped face. "Lorna! Gunner isn't having the room with the attached bathroom. You need to tell him that. He won't listen to me."

"He's only teasing you," I said. "I bet if you ask him nicely, he'll give up his claim on the bedroom."

Gunner strolled in behind Helen, his hands shoved into his dark jeans pockets, and a smug smile on his face. "As to your accusation about my grooming habits, Helen, I don't need to spend much time on my appearance. I look this good naturally. But I still like the idea of an attached bathroom all to myself."

I had to stifle a laugh as Helen stamped her foot.

Gunner grinned at her response. "You're protesting too much about this bathroom. Or maybe you're just getting over excited at the prospect of seeing me hanging out in the kitchen in only my towel."

"As if I'd want to see that." The color on Helen's cheeks increased and she shot a glare at Gunner.

"Give me the attached bathroom and you'll never see me naked." He waggled his brows at Helen.

I shook my head. Part of me wanted to tell them to stop fighting, but I was also enjoying seeing them banter. Every time were together, Helen would get flustered and Gunner would get extra cocky.

They had to like each other. And, although Helen had never said anything to me, she was into Gunner.

I sort of understood her hesitancy. Gunner wasn't her usual type. He lived in jeans and T-shirts, had an East London accent, and worked for the Police. He wasn't Helen's idea of an upper-class gentlemen who wore cravats and spoke with a cut-glass English accent.

Still, there was something between them. The next time we were on our own, I was determined to grill Helen about what she really thought of Gunner Booth. Maybe if she could voice her feelings, she might be less explosive around him.

I smiled up at Zach. I'd already found my dream man, and now we just needed to find a house together.

"Lorna! Tell Gunner he's being stubborn," Helen said, shooting me a pleading look.

"None of you can have any of the bedrooms in this house," I said. "I'm not sure this is the place for us."

Gunner groaned and tipped his head back. "This place is great. There are plenty of rooms, we can move in quickly, and it's less than an hour for me to get to work."

"Lorna's not feeling it," Zach said. "And we've got more places to view before we make a decision."

Helen walked over to me. "More ghosts?"

I looked around the room, not seeing anything otherworldly but knowing something was lurking not far away. "There's something here. I can't put my finger on it, though."

"Have you looked upstairs yet?" Helen asked. "The rooms really are lovely."

I could tell she liked this house but didn't want to pressure me into a decision, knowing how badly ghosts could affect me. "Not yet. We thought we'd let you and Gunner have the bedrooms first." I winked at her.

"In his dreams," she muttered. "Take a look up there. Maybe you'll feel better once you've had a look around everywhere. You can put your mind at rest that there's nothing lurking in the walls."

I looked over at Gunner. He was staring at me with a curious expression on his face. My ghost sensing ability had been mentioned to him, but I'd never told him I could actually see ghosts. It wasn't an easy topic of conversation to bring up, but it was something that needed addressing before we made our living arrangements permanent. I didn't want him to think I was losing my mind when he wandered in and discovered me talking to myself.

"Okay, we'll have a quick look at the bedrooms." I gestured to Zach, and we left Helen, Gunner, and the dogs in the dining room.

"Don't be pressured into buying because Gunner and Helen like the place," Zach said. "Gunner will sleep anywhere. And his work takes him all over the country, so he can't complain about where we're based."

"It is a nice house." I trailed my hand along the antique wooden banister as we walked up the stairs. It needed some redecoration, but other than that it was a solid building. Still, I just wasn't feeling any love for the place.

We checked the first two bedrooms and a bathroom. So far, everything looked ordinary, but the sliver of unease remained with me.

Zach pushed open the next bedroom door and walked in. "This would make a nice main bedroom. We'd get the early morning sunlight in here."

I walked in behind him and stopped, my hand flying to my mouth to stifle a gasp. Standing in the corner of the room was a ghost carrying his head under one arm. It looked like something out of Shakespeare's Macbeth, with a large ruffle around the stump of his neck and long, dark stringy hair on the head.

"What do you think?" Zach turned to me.

"I think it's time to leave," I said, not able to tear my gaze from the ghost.

Zach raised his eyebrows and turned to look at the corner I was staring at. "An unwanted guest?"

I scrubbed my hands up and down my arms. "Yes! One without a head. Or rather, his head is tucked under his arm."

Zach opened his mouth and then snapped it shut. "Right. Let's get out of here. We can carry on the house hunting another day." He grabbed my elbow and hurried me out of the room and back down the stairs.

Helen had her back to Gunner and was staring out the dining room window as we re-entered the room. Gunner was sitting on the floor, his legs stretched out in front of him. Jessie was sitting next to him, enjoying having her ears tickled.

"This isn't the house for us," Zach said.

"Weird vibes upstairs?" Helen turned away from the window.

"The weirdest," I said. "Sorry to disappoint you both."

"It's fine." Gunner got to his feet. "Helen convinced me this isn't going to be our love nest."

"It'll be your final resting place if you keep on with that nonsense," Helen said.

Gunner laughed and held his hand out to her. "You can only resist me for so long, gorgeous."

"I'm planning on making it forever." She played with her blonde curls and then looked away from Gunner.

My phone rang and I pulled it out of my bag. I recognized the number, it was the agency I'd found some of my personal assistant jobs through. I'd been waiting for this call. They were interested in hiring Helen and me to work at a beautiful castle in Yorkshire, home to wild moors and dramatic scenery. I was hoping the jobs would be ours.

"Lorna? It's Josie. I hope you're having a lovely day so far." Her over-the-top bubbly voice sounded too loud.

"Great, thanks. Any news on the Gillan Castle jobs?"

"I'm happy to say Lady Cordelia Babington was most impressed with the resumes she received from you and Helen. She has collected your references and would like you to start immediately." Josie trilled brightly down the phone.

I smiled at Helen and gave her a thumbs-up. "That's great news. We're house hunting not far from Lady Cordelia's castle. We brought our bags just in case she decided to make use of us. We just need to collect them from the hotel we're staying at and we can be with her by the end of the day if that suits."

"She'll be pleased to hear that," Josie said. "I'll email you the details, but you already know everything about the salary and working conditions. Gillan Castle is so beautiful, you'll feel as if you should be paying her for working there."

I shook my head at Josie's enthusiasm. She might be able to work for free, but I needed a salary, and so did Helen, especially if we were both investing in a property with Zach and Gunner. "Tell Lady Cordelia we'll be there within three hours."

"I knew I could rely on you, Lorna," Josie said. "Let's hope this time you get to stay for a while. I'm sorry about what happened at your last place."

I grimaced as I recalled my last employer, Lady Camilla Reynold, who'd been stuck in a gentrified past and not able to see all the weird things going on around her, including her son's unhealthy obsession with his sister, which led to him killing both her and her boyfriend. I'd stuck the job out for eight months as Lady Reynold got used to her son being found guilty for murder and sent for psychiatric evaluation, followed by a lengthy prison sentence.

But there was only so much snapping and coldness Helen and I could bear, and we'd handed in our notices and left.

"We weren't the right fit for Lady Reynold," I said, deciding diplomacy was the most mature route to take. "I'm sure things will be lovely at the castle. We'll fit right in."

"I did have a bit of trouble persuading Lady Cordelia to let Flipper come with you." There was a note of worry in Josie's voice.

"That's not open to negotiation," I said. Flipper went everywhere with me. He was my early warning detection device whenever there was a ghost around. Although it looked like today he was too busy playing with Jessie to let me know there was a headless ghost in one of the bedrooms.

"Don't worry. I persuaded her that Flipper had to come. But I need to warn you, there are a lot of cats in the castle. How does Flipper feel about felines?"

"Flipper loves cats," I said. "He always tries to make friends with them whenever he sees one out on our walks."

"Well, I knew you were an animal lover, so I figured the cats wouldn't be an issue for you."

"A few cats won't be a problem. And Flipper will be happy to have the company when I'm working," I said.

"It sounds perfect for you all," Josie said. "I'm emailing through the details now and will give Lady Cordelia a call to inform her you'll be arriving this afternoon."

We said our goodbyes and I shut off my phone.

"Did you say Gillan Castle?" Gunner asked.

"That's right," I said. "Have you heard of it? It's a gorgeous Grade One listed building in amazing surroundings. When I saw the vacancies come up, I had to go for it."

"Oh, I've heard of it," Gunner said. "Isn't it supposed to be the most haunted castle in the country?"

Zach narrowed his blue eyes and looked at me. "Is that right?"

Helen shushed Gunner and waved her hands at him. "Of course not! Gunner doesn't know what he's talking about. Gillan Castle isn't haunted. I bet they only say that to bring in the tourists."

"It might be a little haunted," I said. "It is over five hundred years old. There will have been a few people who died within the castle walls."

"Were you aware of all these ghosts before you applied for the job?" Zach asked.

"The ghosts won't be a problem." I linked my arm through his elbow. "You know me, I ignore them unless they ask for help."

Gunner's intelligent gaze shot from me to Zach. "I've been meaning to ask you about the ghost thing. How serious is this?"

Zach's arm muscles twitched, and I bit my lip. This could get tricky. What would Gunner think of me when he learned all about my ability?

"That's was another time," Helen said. "All you need to know is that Lorna is amazing and Zach is lucky to have her."

"I am lucky." Zach grinned down at me, the tension easing, and he kissed my forehead.

"I'm not doubting that." Gunner looked at me. "But I keep hearing about ghosts. Do you really believe in them?"

I nodded. "I'll tell you all about it one day."

"That's a story I'm looking forward to." He rubbed the stubble on his chin.

Zach bent down until his mouth was by my ear. "Just make sure you keep out of the ghosts' way in this new job. I don't want you getting in any trouble. If any ghost start causing problems, let me know."

"Are you going to call your ghostbusting friends to come in and help me?" I kissed his cheek. "I won't go looking for any problems. Chances are most of the ghosts in the castle will be old memories, ghosts just acting out the same behavior over and over because that's what they've always done. Ancient history that won't impact on me."

"If there are any missing their heads like the one upstairs," he whispered, "get out of there. You don't always need to go in and save the day."

I shrugged. "I sort of do. You don't meet many people who can see ghosts. And sometimes the ghosts need helping."

Gunner cleared his throat. "Are you sure you don't have time for that ghost story now?"

"No, we don't," Helen said. "Come on, Lorna. We've got a castle to get to."

Chapter 2

The four of us and the dogs piled into Zach's Land Rover, and he drove us back to the hotel we were staying in. It was a quaint place with a thatched roof and ceilings so low Zach had to stoop in the bathroom.

He came with me as I went to collect my bag, shutting the hotel room door softly behind him as I hurried to the closet and emptied the contents into a shoulder bag.

I was excited about starting this new job. I loved working in old buildings. There was always so much history to absorb.

"I've got more details of other houses to read through. Do you want me to view them without you?" Zach asked. "I can take photos and send them over if I like something."

"That sounds good." My thoughts were on my new job as I pulled my main suitcase out of the closet and stuffed my cosmetics bag into it. "You have a look first. If you like it, I can arrange another viewing with you. And we'd better bring along Helen and Gunner as well."

"I'm not sure the two of them living in the same house is such a good idea." Zach caught hold of my arm and spun me into his embrace. "All they do is fight."

I raised my eyebrows. "You do know why that is?"

"They're both as stubborn as each other?"

"Stubborn! That's definitely a family trait."

Zach gave me a mock frown. "It runs in your family as well."

I smacked him lightly on the chest. "They might both be stubborn, but that's not it. They're into each other."

Zach made a choking sound. "You can't be serious. Helen and Gunner?"

"Haven't you seen the way Helen goes red around him?" I asked. "And Gunner starts flexing his biceps and getting all... smoldering."

He cocked an eyebrow. "Gunner smolders?"

I laughed. "I don't think he does, but Helen thinks otherwise."

"Helen only behaves like that because Gunner annoys her so much," Zach said. "And I grew up with the guy, so I know how she feels. He loves to wind people up."

"Nope. I'm certain. Helen gets like that when she likes someone."

"So why doesn't she ask him out?"

I sighed. "Because he doesn't come with his own estate and a closet full of cravats."

Zach laughed as he pushed my hair away from my face. "Would you like to see me in a cravat?"

I chuckled. "What else would you be wearing?"

"Whatever you want me to." He gave my lips a gentle kiss.

"Hmmm. I'll give it some thought."

"And while you're thinking about the cravats, make sure you keep focused on our house hunting."

"I promise, I will," I said. "As soon as we're settled at the castle, I'll get straight on the internet and start looking. And the location of the job is handy. If you find anything, it'll be easy for me to come out after work and do some viewings with you."

"If it weren't for my concerns about all the ghosts in this castle you're going to, I may agree with you," he said.

"I never said there would be lots of ghosts. That's Gunner putting ideas in your head. There might be no ghosts."

"There sounds like there will be more than one ghost, though," Zach said. "It's a spooky old castle. They always come with past."

"But most of the ghosts will be non-threatening," I said. "They won't bother me."

"And if any of them do bother you?"

"I'll set Helen on them."

"What's she going to do? Smack them over the head with a stiletto and tell them to behave themselves?"

"She would if she could see them. And that method works with Gunner," I said. "But seriously, I'll take it easy. It's not fun being bothered by ghosts. And although you seem to think I enjoy it, I wouldn't mind having a normal job for once. One that involves lots of paperwork, filing, and no ghosts."

"So long as you take care of yourself, that's all that concerns me." Zach gave me another kiss and waited as I gathered my final few things, before carrying my bag down the stairs.

We met Helen and Gunner in the hotel lobby. Jessie and Flipper were sitting next to each other by the door, and seemed reluctant to say goodbye. Flipper kept nuzzling Jessie with his nose and gently whining.

I felt the same when it came to Zach. I hated spending too much time apart, but our jobs often called for it. And he had a few tasks to finish at his last place of work before he could start looking for something local.

I'd still see him at the weekends, and we kept in touch by phone. We were used to long distance, but that didn't make it any easier.

Gunner made a grab for Helen just before she got in the car and tried to plant a kiss on her cheek.

She shoved him away. "Keep your hands to yourself."

Gunner placed his hand over his heart and pulled an exaggerated frown. "I was only being friendly. Lorna will let me kiss her goodbye."

I offered him the back of my hand. "Just don't try any of your funny business. Helen's warned me what you're like."

Gunner pressed a kiss to my hand under Zach's watchful gaze. "As if I'd do anything like that. With my baby brother standing next to us, it would be more than my life's worth."

"You'd better believe it," Zach growled. "Lorna's off the market."

My toes curled as Zach became all possessive over me.

Our suitcases were in the back of Helen's car, and Flipper gave Jessie one last nuzzle before climbing onto the back seat and settling himself in for the journey.

I checked the email on my phone, before keying in the information on the GPS to get us to Gillan Castle without getting lost.

I waved goodbye to Zach, Gunner, and Jessie, who stood outside the hotel.

I was looking forward to living with Zach and putting an end to these goodbyes. I was sure it would be fun to live with Helen and Gunner, too. We just needed to find a place that suited us all.

"I can't wait to see what our new home will be like." Helen glanced at the GPS, before heading toward the motorway.

"It's been awhile since we've worked in a castle," I said.

She glanced over at me. "And you're not worried about the possibility of lots of ghosts? I remember when we spent a month in that French château, you got woken several times a night by icy fingered restless spirits. And didn't one of the ghosts trap you in the wine cellar?"

I shuddered as I remembered the horrible four weeks we'd spent in France. Despite the beautiful countryside, fabulous weather, and easy work, I'd been exhausted by the bothersome ghosts. I'd had to hand in my notice, driven out by ghosts who wanted nothing more than to annoy me.

"Maybe the French ghosts just didn't like me," I said. "Gillan Castle will be different."

"And Yorkshire is such a lovely place," Helen said. "You never know, you might even convince me to go out on one of your walks to enjoy the beautiful scenery."

"Are you sure you're feeling all right," I said. "I don't think you've ever volunteered to come walking with me."

"Only if it's sunny," Helen said. "And if there's a pub lunch at the end of it and a big mug of hot chocolate."

I laughed. "I reckon we can get that sorted."

Flipper started snoring as he drifted off to sleep, and I relaxed into my seat and switched on the radio.

We spent the next hour singing along to pop songs in our best out of tune voices.

"So, what's going on with you and Gunner?" I asked as I turned the music down.

"What do you mean?" Helen shot me a sideways glare. "I try to keep out of his way as much as possible. He enjoys teasing me."

"You must hate all that attention."

"And he's too grabby for my liking," she said. "He's all big hands and muscles. He's always invading my personal space."

"That must be so horrible for you," I said. Gunner was a good-looking guy. He shared that family trait with Zach, and I knew that Helen had noticed as well.

The first time they'd met, she'd come over all flustered and started pouting and smoothing her hair. It was classic flirting Helen style.

She let out a sigh and stared at the GPS. "Don't distract me. I don't want to get lost, and we're almost there."

"I'm not distracting you, but I need to know what's going on. We're all going to be living together, after all. I don't want to stumble over you and Gunner having a secret tryst when I come down for hot chocolate and cookies in the middle of the night."

She snorted a laugh. "Nothing's going on. You don't have to worry about anything like that happening."

"Would you like there to be something going on?"

"No! He's not my type."

"How about if we dressed him in a nice suit, gave him a shave, and a house of his own?"

Helen glared at me but then shrugged. "I like his stubble. And he's not hideous to look at."

I clapped my hands together and laughed. "I knew you liked him."

"I don't! I like my men posh with an excellent education. Gunner is neither posh nor well-educated."

"He must have a decent education," I said. "He's a chief superintendent in the police. You don't get there without sitting a few exams."

"Fine, so he's got some brains," Helen said. "But you know I've had this dream ever since I was a little girl. I want to live in a big stately home and be treated like a princess by some rich older man."

"And that's a lovely dream," I said. "Maybe real life will be a bit different. And the trouble with older guys is, well... they're old. You want someone you can have fun with, someone to make you laugh and chase you around the bedroom. You don't want to get stuck with some old guy with a walking frame and a comb-over."

"I don't mean that old! But Gunner's an enormous pain," Helen said. "He's always picking on me."

"Like boys used to do in the playground when you were growing up?"

"Just like that," she said. "He's so childish."

"It's not childish. He's showing that he likes you, just like the boys who used to pull your pigtails. Gunner's teasing is the same thing."

"This is nothing like that," Helen said.

"It's exactly like that," I said. "You two should sit down and have a talk. I bet when you get Gunner on his own, he's completely different."

"I'd be wasting my time," she said. "And it doesn't matter, anyway. I bet I find my prince charming in Gillan Castle. There could be some lonely gorgeous bachelor drifting around the estate just waiting for me to arrive."

"And if there isn't a dashing prince?" I asked. "Will you consider Gunner then?"

"I wouldn't consider Gunner Booth if he was the only man left on Earth."

I snorted out a laugh. "He's not that bad."

"I suppose if we did get together and got married—"

"Hold up! You hated him a few minutes ago."

She grinned. "I still do, but, if we got serious, and you married Zach and I married Gunner, that would make us sisters."

I grinned. "We're as good as sisters as it is."

"We are, but I guess that is one good reason to consider Gunner. Anyway, I'm not sure he's the marrying kind. He's more of a flirt like mad, get what he wants, and then run for the hills sort of guy."

"You should give him a go," I said. "It would get rid of all the frustrating tension in the air every time the two of you are in the same room."

"I'm only tense when I'm around Gunner because I'm waiting for him to start winding me up," she said. "That's the only tension I can imagine you're referring to."

"Remember what I said about boys and pigtails."

"Do be quiet," she said. "This is the exit we want. I need to concentrate so I don't drive us into a ditch."

I smiled at Helen, but decided not to press her any more on the matter of Gunner. They'd get there eventually, and it would be fun watching them bickering until they figured out their feelings.

And as for this job, I had a good feeling about it. It would work out this time. There might be a few ghosts in the castle, but they'd be happy to drift around without getting in our way. They'd have plenty of tourists to bother and wouldn't even notice me.

I drummed my fingers on the seat. Was I being foolishly optimistic? I hoped not.

"I love this song!" Helen turned the sound up on the radio and started an off-key rendition of the theme tune from the movie St Elmo's Fire.

I grinned and joined in. No, I wasn't being naive. We were going to love Gillan Castle.

Chapter 3

"This must be the place." Helen stopped the car.

We both stared wide-eyed at the enormous sandstone castle in front of us. It was like something out of a medieval fantasy and looked more like a fortress than a private residence.

Gillan Castle was privately owned, but the family, the Babingtons, opened some of the castle to the public. They were allowed to walk through velvet roped-off rooms and admire the finery the family had acquired over generations.

The gardens were also extensive, consisting of twenty-five acres, containing a maze, a formal rose garden, and an elaborate vista of neatly trimmed hedge animals.

Helen nudged me with her elbow and showed me the screen on her phone. "There's a dungeon in the castle."

"I expect they only use it for staff who misbehave."

She tutted as she scrolled through the information on her phone. "And they have rooms dedicated to different kings as well. Oh, and there's also a torture chamber."

"That must have been set up for you," I said.

"Oh dear. And there's something else." Helen shot me a worried look.

"What could be worse than a dungeon and a torture chamber?" I was still admiring the turrets and the flags as they waved over the top of the impressive roof.

"It says here that it's one of the most haunted places in the country." Helen grimaced at me. "I hate to admit it, but Gunner was right."

"Don't let him hear you say that. He'll hold it over you forever."

"We'll have to hope the ghosts are all friendly." Helen put her phone away. "And they don't need your help."

"Old ghosts don't usually need help," I said. "It's the newly deceased ones, the ones who ran into trouble not so long ago and have issues that need to be resolved that are the most difficult. I don't mind encountering a few thirteenth-century ghosts in the dungeon. And even if I do, there's not much I'll be able to do to help them. If they were killed or came to a grisly end, then their killer is long since dead. There's no point in them hanging out here and getting in our way."

"Of course. You're right. These ghosts won't be a bother. Let's get our bags and go take a look around." Helen parked the car around the side of the castle and let Flipper out.

We pulled our suitcases out of the trunk, before walking past the public entrance and to the private access which read *staff only*.

As we waited for the door to open, a large black cat strolled past.

Flipper's ears pricked up and he took a step toward the cat.

The cat's hackles instantly raised and it hissed at Flipper.

I petted Flipper's head. "Better luck next time. Not all cats love you. You might look a bit scary to them."

Flipper whined and looked back at the cat who was now spitting and stepping backward slowly, its narrowed green eyes not leaving Flipper, just waiting for him to start chasing.

"I meant to tell you, there's a lot of cats living in the castle," I said to Helen.

"Most likely to keep the mice and rats down," she said. "These places always have a problem with vermin."

"Josie didn't say why there are so many here," I said. "Maybe the owner just likes cats."

"Well, I definitely prefer cats to rats, so I don't mind a few cute fuzz balls hanging around the place. Although I'm never a fan of clearing up their mess when they bring up a hairball."

The staff door opened, and a middle-aged woman with bright red cheeks looked out at us. She wore a black dress, covered by a red apron with dusty handprints smeared on it. "May I help you?"

"I'm Lorna Shadow and this is Helen Holiday," I said. "We're here to start work for Lady Cordelia."

"Are you the new personal assistant and seamstress?" The woman smiled at us both. "I'm Daphne Jones, house cook. Do come in." She stood back from the door and pushed it open wider, gesturing at us as she did so.

We both nodded a greeting as we walked into a dimly lit corridor with brightly patterned floor tiles. The pleasing smell of baking bread drifted toward us.

"Lady Cordelia said to expect you," Daphne said. "Our butler is off sick, so I've been running around doing two jobs. I'm a bit behind on the cooking, and things are manic here today. The castle is open for visitors, and Julius, Lady Cordelia's son, has just said he wants guests for afternoon tea. How am I supposed to rustle up two dozen scones out of thin air? Not to mention the sandwiches and little cakes he likes. That boy tries my patience sometimes."

"I can help with that," Helen said. "I love cooking."

Daphne's dark brown eyes widened and she smiled at Helen. "I think I've just been sent an angel. Can you really help?"

"Of course!" She smiled at Daphne. "Give me five minutes to put my bags away and I'm all yours."

"Well, it looks like Lady Cordelia did a good thing hiring the two of you. Let me show you to your rooms and then we can have some tea while we bake."

"That sounds good," I said, hoping I wasn't being included in the offer to help with the baking. My skills when it came to baked goods revolved around eating them, not making them.

We followed Daphne along the corridor and down a short flight of concrete stone steps. We turned right and walked along another corridor.

"All staff have their own quarters down here," Daphne said. "It's comfortable enough and it's always lovely and warm. You both get your own room and there are attached bathrooms in each of them." She stopped by a closed door, unlocked it, and passed me the key. "This one is yours. Use anything you like that's in there."

I poked my head inside the room and saw a large double bed covered in a baby-pink bedspread. There were a several pillows on the bed and a warm looking blanket. There was also a dark wooden closet and a chest of drawers.

"This all looks great," I said.

"Helen's room is right next to yours." Daphne unlocked the next door and gave Helen her own key.

After a quick inspection of Helen's room, which was similar to mine, and putting our bags away, we followed

Daphne back up the stairs and into an open plan kitchen. Several other staff hurried to and fro, opening and closing wooden cabinets and checking the stove. There was a large well used table in the center of the kitchen that must seat twenty people.

Daphne shooed a stripy tabby cat out the back door, before shutting it. "You'll get used to the cats. They turn up everywhere. They're lovely, but I can't risk getting cat fur in the food."

"The owner must be a fan of cats." I sat at the kitchen table next to Helen.

"Lady Cordelia isn't a big fan," Daphne said. "Her late husband, Leopold, was. Everyone called him Leo, and it suited him. He absolutely adored cats and picked up every stray he could find. It's funny, they all seemed to know to come here when they wanted a good feed and a cuddle. There's a cat sanctuary on the grounds, and we have staff looking after them full time."

"A cat sanctuary, how adorable," Helen said. "I always admire people who take in unwanted animals."

"Leo had a big heart. He was such a soft touch when it came to any animal in need. Cats were always his big weakness," Daphne said.

"Late husband? How did Leo die?" I asked.

"Oh! It's such a sad story. He was suffocated in his sleep by a cat," Daphne said.

"That's awful!" I resisted the urge to check over my shoulder, expecting to see Leo's ghost lurking behind me.

"Exactly how many cats have you got here?" Helen stood and rolled up her sleeves, before tying the apron Daphne gave her around her trim waist.

"I've lost count," Daphne said. "There must be at least fifty cats in the sanctuary."

"Fifty!" I looked at Flipper who sat patiently by my feet, taking in his new surroundings. "You're going to have lots of furry new friends to play with. I hope Jessie doesn't get jealous when she comes for a visit."

"Is your dog good with cats?" Daphne asked. "He'll need to be if he's going to stay here. They run the place."

"He won't be a problem," I said. "Flipper stays by my side most of the time. He's my assistance dog, you see."

"What does he assist you with?" Daphne pulled out flour and sugar from the cupboard.

"Lorna sometimes faints," Helen said.

"Oh dear! I hope it's nothing serious." Daphne gave me a concerned look.

"It's nothing to worry about," I said. "Flipper always tips me off before I get dizzy." That was my story, and I was sticking to it.

"I'm sure you'll fit right in," Daphne said. "And I bet Flipper likes treats as well. I do enjoy baking, and he'd be welcome to a little cake or two if he gets hungry."

"We all like treats." I grinned at Daphne.

She placed cups on the table and then handed me an empty teapot. "You make the tea while we do the cooking."

"No! Let me." Helen grabbed the teapot out of my hand. She knew better than to let me loose on making the tea. It either ended up stewed or anaemic.

Daphne raised her eyebrows. "Make sure to warm the pot first."

"I always do," Helen said. "I warm the pot, rinse it out, warm it again, and then empty it and make the tea."

"That's just how I do it." Daphne smiled at Helen. "The two of us are going to get along just fine."

I was enjoying my first sip of perfectly brewed tea when the kitchen door opened. A willowy woman with ash blonde hair and blue eyes walked in. She exuded good taste and refinement. I knew instantly it must be our new employer.

"We have guests?" The woman's gaze shifted from me to Helen, who was dusted in flour and had a blob of strawberry jelly on her hand.

"Your Ladyship. I should have brought Helen and Lorna to meet you." Daphne rinsed off her hands and dried them on a dishcloth. "I got a bit carried away making scones and treats for Master Julius."

Lady Cordelia stepped forward. "I see Daphne has been getting you to work straight away. She's good at doing that. She keeps this place running."

I stood and shook hands with Lady Cordelia, and Helen held up her flour-covered hands and simply nodded.

"I showed them to their rooms and they said they were only too happy to help," Daphne said. "What with Alfred being off sick, I'm running around like a headless chicken here."

Lady Cordelia raised her hands. "That's fine, Daphne. You're welcome to make use of them. So long as neither of you mind getting stuck in right away."

"We don't mind," I said. "And it's been a nice introduction to the castle."

"I suppose it must have been." Lady Cordelia looked at the empty cup in my hand.

There was a scratching sound on the kitchen door. Daphne opened it to reveal three identical looking black cats. They charged into the kitchen and ran around, their tails up, eyeing the countertops.

"Don't you dare let them up near the food, Daphne." Lady Cordelia grabbed a cloth and flapped it at the cats, who scattered in all directions. "Those cats get everywhere. I even found one on my bed the other day, and I always keep my bedroom door shut. Sometimes, I think they have magical powers and are able to sneak through walls."

"You don't like having the cats around?" I asked.

"They were my late husband's obsession, not mine. They leave fur everywhere."

"Why did your husband like cats so much?" I asked. "Daphne was saying there are fifty living here."

Lady Cordelia flapped out the cloth she'd grabbed and set it over the back of a chair. "Honestly, what Leo used to do was a mystery to me. Now, perhaps we can meet over dinner and discuss your real work duties in more detail. We dine at seven."

"That's very kind of you. We're both ready to start work whenever you want us to," I said.

Lady Cordelia eyed the mound of warm scones that appeared from the oven.

"Would you like one?" Daphne asked, a twinkle in her dark eyes. "They're for Master Julius and his friends, but I always make extra."

Lady Cordelia smiled and swiped a scone. "Just the one. I can never resist your cooking."

Daphne blushed and smiled. "I'm only doing my job."

"I'll see you ladies at dinner." Lady Cordelia sashayed out of the kitchen, pulling apart the scone and popping a piece into her mouth as she did so.

Daphne walked over to the table and leaned against it. "She's not a bad employer. Although she can be a bit scary if you mess up. If you work hard, she likes you. I've been here five years and never once thought about leaving. She pays well and offers good accommodation. Once you get past her airs and graces, she can be quite a laugh, especially since she found herself a toy boy. He's brought a sparkle to her eyes."

"Lady Cordelia has a toy boy?" Helen chose her own scone and sat back at the table.

"Oh yes. He's a good-looking one as well," Daphne said. "I expect you'll meet Sebastien over dinner. She gets all soppy when she's around him. He's so different from the late Lord Babington. He doesn't come from a wealthy family, but he moves in the right social circles. He caught Lady Cordelia's eye and they've been together ever since. There's even a rumor she might marry him. Although I'm not sure what the children will think about that."

"Lady Cordelia has more than one son?" I asked.

"A daughter as well," Daphne said. "Tabitha. She's a strange one. I try to keep out of the way."

"Why do you think she's strange?"

"She never eats cake! That's not natural in my eyes. Who doesn't like cake?"

"That is odd." I smiled as I looked at the scones. "What else is weird about her?"

"I can't put my finger on it," Daphne said. "She seems lovely on the surface, but there's something just not right about her. Maybe it's me being daft. It's probably my hormones making me think something is strange."

"I think hormones are a very reliable source of information," Helen said. "Mine never let me down. They always ping when trouble is looming."

Daphne joined us and passed around the scones and topped up our cups. "We deserve some of these."

I smiled as I bit into my warm, sweet scone. Gillan Castle was definitely being good to me so far.

Half an hour later, we were stuffed full of delicious scones and it was time to leave and discover more about the castle. We said our goodbyes to Daphne and headed out of the kitchen.

Helen had her gaze focused on her phone as she read out more information about the castle. She didn't see a sleek gray cat who crossed her path until it was too late. She tumbled to the floor with a surprised yelp, her phone flying out of her hand.

The cat hissed at Helen and fled away along the corridor.

"Ouch! I'm going off cats." Helen rubbed her knee and looked up at me as she grabbed her phone off the floor.

I wasn't paying her any attention. Flipper was whining and pawing at my feet as my bones chilled and my flesh goose bumped. I swallowed the irrational fear I felt every time I stumbled across a ghost. And there was one very close by. All my senses tingled in nervous anticipation.

"Hello! Your best friend has fallen over," Helen said. "I could do with some sympathy. And any chance you can give me a hand up?"

I nodded and held out my hand, but my gaze remained fixed to the end of the corridor, where the ghost of an old man had just materialized.

Chapter 4

Helen grumbled as she got to her feet and brushed down her tan dress. "What's got you so distracted?"

Flipper dashed toward the ghost and stared at it for a few seconds, before running back to me and checking I was doing okay.

"We've got company," I said.

"Our first ghost?" she asked. "I'm surprised you haven't seen one already. This *is* supposed to be the most haunted place in the country. What's the ghost doing? Is it a creepy one? An ancient knight? No! A grizzled warrior?"

"Nothing like that. He's just looking at us, and he's not scary," I said.

"Is he an old looking ghost?"

"Well, he's got a white beard," I said. "He looks a bit like Richard Attenborough."

"That's not what I meant," Helen said. "Is he from centuries ago, wearing chainmail like an old-fashioned knight?"

"No. He looks like a modern sort of ghost," I said. "He's got a suit on. And you'll be pleased to know, he's wearing a cravat."

"Ooooh! He sounds like my sort of ghost," she said. "Is he paying you any attention?"

"He is," I said. "And prepare to feel cold, because he's coming this way."

The ghost drifted along the corridor, slowing as a cat darted out in front of him. He bent and attempted to stroke the cat, but it spat at him and dashed away. The ghost frowned and shook his head, before drawer closer.

"He's here." My skin goose bumped again as the temperature lowered.

"Is he giving you any clue as to who he is?" Helen asked.

The ghost turned his attention to Helen and he bowed before turning and doing the same to me.

"I think you'd like him if you could see him," I said. He's got old-fashioned manners."

"That's a good start," she said. "Anything else?"

"He's pointing up the stairs. I guess he wants us to follow him somewhere," I said.

The ghost nodded and drifted past us, causing us both to shudder. We turned and followed the ghost up the stairs into the main hallway of the castle. This area appeared to be out of bounds to visitors because no one was around. It was full of antique furniture and dozens of oil paintings.

The ghost drifted halfway along the hallway, before stopping by a painting and pointing at it.

I hurried over and read the small gold plaque on the painting. "This must be our ghost. Leopold Babington." I looked up at the stately figure in the painting, which showed a white-bearded, white-haired man in a smart pale suit. He had a small pot belly and a walking cane in one hand. His expression in the painting was firm and his blue eyes looked bright and warm.

"That's Lady Cordelia's late husband," Helen said. "What's he doing still hanging around the castle?"

I looked at Leo. "Do you want to tell us why you're here?"

Leo nodded and turned as a white cat strolled into the hallway. He moved toward the cat and it instantly bristled and narrowed its eyes before darting away, its fur bushed up around it.

"You're scaring the cats," I said. "They might not know what to make of a ghost. When you get near me, I feel cold. You could have that same effect on them. And you know how much cats like to be warm."

Leo shook his head sadly and his gaze followed the cat as it hurried along the corridor and out through the flap in the door.

"You must love animals as much as I do." I looked down at Flipper and stroked his head.

Leo nodded and smiled at Flipper, before holding his hand out to him.

Flipper sniffed the air where Leo's hand was and gave a gentle whine before looking back at me.

"Flipper likes you too," I said. "That's always a good sign. So, how can we help you? Did you leave something behind when you died? Any last requests you want us to pass onto family members?"

Leo scratched his beard and pointed in the direction the cat had gone.

"Is it something outside?" I asked.

Before he could attempt to communicate any more, the door at the end of the hallway was pushed open. A younger, taller version of Leo strolled through. He was followed by a dark-haired, slim, classically handsome man in a checked waistcoat and dark blue suit.

"And I said to her, if she'd just wear her skirt two inches shorter, I was sure she'd get the promotion she wanted." The younger version of Leo laughed loudly and took a sip from a silver hip flask he held. "I couldn't understand it when she slapped me across the face. I was complimenting her great legs, that was all."

The man in the checked waistcoat nodded but a grimace passed across his face. "I have an idea why she might have slapped you."

"Women are too sensitive these days." The man looked in our direction and smiled. "It looks like we've got company."

Leo vanished through the wall, leaving Helen and me none the wiser as to why he was still in the castle.

I walked toward the two men and held my hand out. "I'm Lady Cordelia's new personal assistant, Lorna Shadow."

"Charmed. I'm Montgomery Babington, Leo's younger brother." He pumped my hand firmly, his fingers caressing my palm as he did so. His confident gaze ran over me before turning to Helen.

I introduced Helen and then looked at the man in the checked waistcoat.

"I'm not a Babington," he said as he waved away Montgomery's offer of the hip flask.

"You're definitely not," Montgomery said. "But I expect you will be soon enough. Cordelia isn't going to change her name once the two of you get married."

The man shook his head at Montgomery. "I'm Sebastien Arden."

"Cordelia's bit of stuff," Montgomery said. He laughed as Sebastien scowled at him. "Oh, come on. Everyone knows it's true. You're half her age and twice as attractive. I wonder what you see in her."

"Cordelia's a very attractive older woman. Her maturity is appealing," Sebastien said. "It's not all about looks, anyway."

"I don't know what else it could be about," Montgomery said. He looked over at us. "My friends call me Monty. I insist you ladies be my friends. It gets so boring around here. It'll be good to have more company to liven things up."

"We're here to work, not entertain you," Helen said.

"Just looking at you is entertainment enough." Montgomery grinned broadly at Helen.

She crossed her arms over her chest and glared at him.

Sebastien smiled at Helen. "I like your dress. It makes your hair color look really pretty."

Helen's glare softened and she stroked her hands over her dress. "Thanks. It's one of my favorites."

"Stop flirting you old hound. I reckon Helen's a feisty one. Make sure you don't get on the wrong side of her." Montgomery's grin only widened as Helen huffed at him.

Sebastien shot me and Helen an apologetic look. "Ignore Monty. Cordelia won't like him pestering her new staff."

"And she won't like you much for thinking you're going to have fun with them either," Montgomery said. "Besides, everything I do annoys Cordelia. She'd ban me from this place if she could. Lucky for me that Leo insisted I could stay for as long as I like. She can't kick me out if she wanted to. Leo was always good at getting the lawyers involved and making things watertight. If he hadn't done so, Cordelia would have turned this place into an amusement park to make a bit of extra money."

"How much of the castle is open to the public?" I asked.

"About half of it," Montgomery said. "Have you had the grand tour yet?"

"We've seen the downstairs staff area," I said. "That's about it."

"Well then, we've got time for a tour before dinner." Montgomery tucked my hand through his elbow. "Let's show you around and welcome you to your new home."

Despite Montgomery being a little on the sleazy side, I got the impression it was the alcohol from his hip flask doing the talking more than anything else.

I accepted his offer, and we all walked along the hallway and into an enormous room full of glass cabinets.

Flipper following closely behind, his nose glued to the carpet.

"This is the Witch Room," Montgomery said.

"Why's it called that?" I asked.

"Rumor has it that anyone who tries to steal from the castle gets cursed by our local witch."

"I imagine that would put a lot of people off of getting light-fingered." I cast a cautious look around the room, but didn't feel anything otherworldly. Not that I believed in witches, but then most people didn't believe in ghosts, and I could see them.

"This room is a mess," Sebastien said. "There's a dummy of a witch over there, but then there's all the photographs about the trip your great-uncle made to Everest. There's even one of the sleds he used on his trip covered by an old tarp. That shouldn't be mixed in with a load of witch memorabilia. Not unless you're trying to sell your relative as some ancient mystical warlock."

"He'd shoot you if you called him that," Montgomery said. "It's a shame he's not alive to chase you around the castle."

Sebastien chuckled. "I'd have liked to have met him. He sounded like fun."

"He was." Montgomery look around. "But you're right, it does need a good sort out in here. People love the mismatch of stuff, though. They spend hours gazing into these cabinets. They're full of witch stones."

"Witch stones?" Helen asked. "What are they?"

"People used to lay them on their doorstep to ward off evil and keep the witch from escaping the castle and coming to jinx them." Montgomery took me over to the next display. "And see this massive bowl in here? It was used for pouring boiling oil on unwelcome visitors when the castle was under siege, which I believe it has been on several occasions. Though never when I've been at home." He laughed at his own joke before showing us the next room.

Montgomery and Sebastien led us around the armory, a medieval courtyard, and the Great Hall, which was a vast space covered with weapons and trophies and had several original twelfth-century arrow slits carved into the thick stone walls.

We were also treated to a look in two rooms dedicated to late kings of England, all luxurious in their finery with velvet-covered wall hangings and deluxe four-poster beds. We were introduced to the main museum, another room crammed full of curiosities, and then shown the chapel, a place that was off-limits to the public during family services.

The next room was full of prehistoric finds, old flint axes, primitive tools, and maps showing the dispersal of modern humans across the country.

"This next bit is my favorite," Montgomery said. "I hope you two don't get spooked easily."

I shot Helen a knowing look. "Not much scares us."

"I'm glad to hear it." Montgomery pulled open the door with a flourish. "Welcome to the castle's torture chamber."

I descended a short flight of stone stairs, the air getting colder with every step, and walked into a stone chamber.

Helen hurried past me and grabbed a vicious looking set of thumb screws. "I bet you can do some damage with these."

I nodded as I inspected an executioner's block, complete with its own basket to catch heads. There were worryingly realistic dark stains on the wooden chopping block.

"All of these are the real deal," Montgomery said. "They've been used in this castle. You'll be happy to know we only have them on display now. Although Cordelia would probably like to use them on people who don't do what she wants."

"He's exaggerating," Sebastien said. "Cordelia has a gentle nature."

"Compared to a pit bull, she does," Montgomery said.

"Look at this! It would make anyone talk." Helen opened an iron maiden, its dull interior spikes looking long and menacing.

I ran my fingers over a scold's bridle, which, according to the plaque next to it, was used on gossips who didn't know when to keep their mouths shut. "It's an impressive haul of torture devices."

Helen joined me and we looked around the rest of the room. "It's not so scary."

"It would be if you were inside the scold's bridle or the iron maiden," Montgomery said. "Can I tempt you to try them?"

"Not likely." Helen frowned at him.

"Just imagine all the horrible things that happened down here to our enemies," Montgomery said. "All those people who tried to break into the castle and steal from us. Most castles have rooms like this. It's only right you punish people who do things you don't want them to."

"You don't have to torture them," Helen said. "Simply telling them not to do it again should be enough."

"Not when they're trying to raze your castle to the ground it isn't," Montgomery said. "We need a few more instruments of torture in here. I always liked the look of those balls with spikes on them, the kind you swing at your enemy when in battle. They'd leave a nasty bruise."

Helen shook her head. "We've seen enough of this room."

Montgomery downed the contents of his hip flask. "It's almost time for dinner, anyway. Let's see what Daphne has rustled up for us this evening. She always puts on a good spread."

"We'll meet you in there," I said. "We just want to freshen up before dinner and unpack."

Montgomery shrugged. "As you like. Although you both look decent enough in what you're already wearing. We don't go for anything fancy here, unless Cordelia dresses you." He looked at Sebastien and winked.

Sebastien glowered in response and tugged at the hem of his tailored suit jacket.

We said our goodbyes, and I grabbed Helen's elbow and hurried us toward our rooms.

"I thought we might get a chance to speak to Leo before dinner," I said. "He was trying to tell me something just before Montgomery and Sebastien arrived. He disappeared through the wall, though. I guess he didn't want to do the castle tour."

"Leo must have seen those rooms thousands of times when he was alive," Helen said. "Isn't it a shame the way he died? Suffocated by a cat. I've never heard that happening before."

"That could be why he's still here," I said. "Maybe a cat didn't smother him."

"You think Leo could have been murdered?"

"Let's hope not. But he's hanging around the castle for a reason."

She grinned at me. "How exciting! This just got interesting."

Chapter 5

I entered my bedroom and discovered a fat ginger cat sitting on the end of the bed, his large bushy tail tucked around him, covering his nose. One yellow eye opened and he regarded us calmly.

"I wonder if we both get a cat in our bedrooms." Helen walked over to my bed and sat down, before offering her fingers to the cat to sniff.

He inspected her hand carefully, before settling his head back on my bed.

"He certainly seems at home there," I said. "How did he get in, though? The door was shut."

"The window's open," Helen said. "Maybe he jumped in and decided to have a nap."

Flipper wandered over to the bed and stared at the ginger cat.

The cat lifted his head and blinked at Flipper.

"Do you think Flipper has found a new friend?" Helen watched their interaction with interest.

"That is one enormous tomcat," I said. "Flipper had better watch his nose if he doesn't want to get it scratched. Not all cats like dogs."

The cat hopped up, stretched his back and curled himself around Helen several times, weaving between her arms and butting his head against her side.

"He's a cutie," she said. "If you don't want him in your room, I'll have him."

"Cats decide where they want to go," I said. "But if he's willing, you're welcome to him. Flipper usually shares the bed with me. The three of us on one bed might be a bit of a squash if he stay the night."

The cat jumped off the bed and walked over to me, his tail in the air. He sat at my feet and gave the sweetest meow I'd ever heard.

I bent and stroked his head, hearing a deep purr rumble through his chest. "He is quite charming."

Flipper whined, and looked up to see him standing by the door, a glum expression on his face.

"Don't worry. You're still my favorite," I said. "You always will be."

Flipper paced backward and forward, his attention no longer on me.

The cat backed away rapidly, his eyes also on the door, just where Flipper was looking.

The air chilled and Leo popped through the door.

Flipper danced on his paws, and the cat moved to stand next to him, his fur bristling all over his body and his eyes narrowed.

"I'm guessing Leo's here," Helen said as she watched Flipper and the cat.

Leo tried to stroke the ginger cat, but he spat at him and backed away. Leo shook his head, his mouth turning down as he watched the cat grow fluffier, making it look like he had a ginger afro.

"He was trying to pet the cat," I said to Helen.

"Poor Leo," she said. "It must be so hard for him, not being able to interact with the cats. It sounds like he was fond of them."

Leo nodded at Helen's comment and drifted slowly toward us.

I sat next to Helen on the bed and looked at Leo. "So, this is how it works; I can see you and I know you see and hear me, but I can't hear you. You're going to need to be inventive if you want to communicate with us."

Leo scratched a hand through his beard and nodded.

"I'm guessing you're still here for a reason," I said. "Have you got something you want to pass onto a loved one?"

He glanced at the ginger cat, who was now less fluffy and was licking a paw, his gaze still not leaving Leo.

"Does it have something to do with your cats?" I asked. "I hear you have quite a collection here. Did you want to leave them some money so you know they'll be well cared for?"

Leo shook his head.

"If it's not about the cats, could it be about Lady Cordelia?" I asked. "Are you unhappy she's found somebody new?"

"I hope you aren't the jealous type," Helen said. "It's only fair that your wife isn't alone."

Leo looked down at his ring finger and shook his head.

I glanced at Helen. "It's not the cats and it's not his wife." I looked back at Leo. "We met your brother this evening. Has your being here got something to do with him?"

Leo shrugged and his bottom lip jutted out.

I let out a sigh. "I'm not sure he knows why he's here."

"How does Leo think he died?" Helen asked.

"Good point." I looked at Leo. "What do you think happened to you? Daphne said you were smothered by a cat when you were asleep."

He floated closer to the bed and pointed at a pillow, his hand squashing down on the middle of it.

"He's trying to do something with my pillow," I said.

"Do you think he was smothered by a pillow and not a cat?" Helen asked.

I grimaced. "I hope not. What a horrible way to die."

Leo pointed at Helen and nodded.

"Oh dear. It looks like you're right," I said.

Leo flopped onto the bed and rolled around a bit.

I had to stifle a laugh as he flailed his arms and legs around.

"What's going on?" Helen asked. "I can feel the bed moving. What's Leo doing?"

"Re-enacting his last moments," I said. "At least, I think that's what he's doing."

Leo climbed off the bed and straightened his cravat and jacket. He pointed over at the ginger cat.

"He keeps going back to the cats," I said. "If someone did smother Leo in his sleep, maybe a cat witnessed what happened."

"That's not going to be any help," Helen said. "Or are you going to suggest a cat goes under questioning in a murder trial?"

I smacked her arm. "Of course not. But Leo thinks it's important."

"Maybe he keeps pointing at the cats because he was obsessed with them when he was alive," she said. "You often hear about mad cat ladies, those women who give up on love and surround themselves with dozens of substitute fur babies, but you don't often hear about men who get obsessed like that."

"Are you ever tempted to go down that path?" I asked. "You have been single a long time."

"Hey! I haven't given up on love yet." She glared at me. "And I'm not over the hill either. There are plenty of men out there who'll consider me a catch."

"Of course, they will." I looked at Flipper and smiled fondly. I could understand why people got so obsessed with their animals. Flipper was *my* fur baby, and I wouldn't have it any other way.

"What do you want to do about Leo?" Helen asked. "Aren't you supposed to be keeping out of the way of all the ghosts in the castle?"

"I don't think Leo will be a problem. He looks like a sweet old man to me, and he's much more interested in his cats than anything else. Maybe he simply doesn't want to leave them."

"He also won't want to leave if he was smothered and someone got away with killing him," Helen said. "And if he was smothered to death, it's only right that we help him."

Leo was trying to get closer to the big ginger cat. The cat skipped out of his reach every time Leo got close enough to brush his fingers down his spine.

"Maybe a family member got annoyed with Leo's devotion to the cats," I said.

Leo pointed at me and nodded.

"He agrees with that idea," I said.

"Since Lady Cordelia had so much to gain from Leo's death, and she's got herself a hot new lover, we should start with her as our main suspect," Helen said.

"You could be right. And she didn't act like much of a grieving widow when we met. Okay, let's do some discreet looking around and see what we discover. But keep it discreet. We don't want to lose our jobs before we've even started them."

"Discreet is my middle name," Helen said.

"I thought it was flirt." That comment earned me a smack on the arm.

"I never flirt, unless the guy is extremely gorgeous and single" she said. "Now, let's hurry up and go see what we've got for dinner."

Chapter 6

I had a quick freshen up, and met Helen outside my room, before we headed up the stairs to find the dining room.

We were accompanied by the cat, who I'd decided to nickname Big Ginge, and Leo, who drifted along beside us, occasionally pointing at pictures on the wall.

Laughter alerted me to what was most likely the dining room. I pushed open the door, to discover an antique-blue room, with a black fireplace and white mantel surround. Gold candlesticks dotted numerous surfaces, and the center of the room was dominated by a large, dark wooden table, set for dinner.

"Ah! Glad you found us." Sebastien hurried over and smiled. "We didn't get around to showing you this part of the house. This is the family only part, so no tourists allowed in here."

"Not a problem," I said. "It was easy enough to find."

"I wanted to say sorry about Monty's earlier behavior," Sebastien said. He glanced over his shoulder as Montgomery laughed loudly. "He's a decent enough guy, but a bit too fond of the old drink. He's been like it ever since Leo died. I think it hit him harder than he cares to admit."

"It must be his way of coping." I looked over to where Montgomery stood. He had an empty whiskey glass in one hand and was studying a number of bottles of alcohol in front of him.

"Now you've made me feel bad for snapping at him," Helen said.

"That won't bother Monty," Sebastien said. "And if he likes you, nothing will put him off. Just a word of warning, he does like blondes."

"Perhaps I'm not available to be liked," Helen said.

"Of course not. A lovely girl like you must have a queue of suitors waiting to take her out," he said.

Helen blushed and smiled. "I can see why Lady Cordelia likes you."

Sebastien ducked his head. "We get on well. She's a nice lady. A little demanding at times, but then she's used to getting her own way, given she's now in charge of this entire castle."

"Do you mind me asking about her late husband?" I kept half an eye on Leo as he drifted around the room, his fingers trailing over objects as if he was remembering his time here when he was alive.

"That's a bit of a sad story," Sebastien said. "You've probably heard the rumors."

"Tell us anyway," Helen said.

"Well, as you may have noticed, there are lots of cats around." Sebastien lowered his voice and leaned closer.

"Daphne said there's a cat sanctuary somewhere on the grounds," I said.

"That's right. Leo was mad about cats. He even named his daughter Tabitha, because it was his favorite cat's name."

"I bet she loved that," Helen said.

"Actually, it suits her," Sebastien said. "Anyway, Leo always had a cat on the bed when he slept at night. And one night, the cat decided to sleep on Leo's face and suffocated him."

"That's so sad," Helen said.

I looked at Leo. Maybe he'd been mistaken about how he died. He hadn't been suffocated by a human, after all.

"I doubt Leo would have known what was going on when it happened," Sebastien said. "He had a condition called sleep apnoea, which gave him trouble with his breathing. And the cat certainly wouldn't have had a clue what it was doing. It probably got cold and decided to snuggle next to its favorite person."

"How old was Leo when he died?" Helen asked.

"He was about fifteen years older than Cordelia. That made him sixty when he died, so he wasn't an old man," Sebastien said. "Cordelia was all for getting rid of every single cat after it happened. Then she calmed down and realized the cat didn't do it deliberately."

"I'm sure you're right about that," I said.

Sebastien looked toward the dining room door, where quick high-heeled footsteps were approaching. "Cordelia doesn't like anybody talking about Leo. It's best you don't mention this conversation. We don't want to upset her."

"Sebastien, darling!" Lady Cordelia dashed into the dining room and grabbed hold of his arm. "I was thinking you'd abandoned me. Why didn't you come and find me?"

Sebastien kissed Lady Cordelia on the cheek. It was an oddly formal gesture. "I've been counting down the minutes since I left you, just waiting to return to your side."

"You're such a romantic." Lady Cordelia neatened Sebastien's jacket, a small frown on her lips. "I thought you were going to wear the new tweed jacket I got you?"

"I decided to have it altered," he said. "The tailor has it. I'll wear it another time."

"It'll makes you look even more handsome," Lady Cordelia said. "As if that's possible." She giggled like a schoolgirl, not seeming to have noticed we were standing right next to Sebastien.

"I'll fix you a drink." He gestured toward the drinks cabinet.

Lady Cordelia's spine stiffened as she locked gazes with Montgomery, who was still pondering over the drinks. "Monty. I hope you haven't been leading Sebastien astray again?"

"I do my best to," he said, not raising his gaze. "He's a hard one to corrupt, though. He barely drinks, doesn't smoke, and seems worryingly attached to you. I suggested we go to London and spend an evening at the Gaslight Gentlemen's Club, but he didn't think much of that idea. We settled on a boozy dinner here instead."

"Of course I didn't." Sebastien shook his head as he fixed Lady Cordelia's drink. "What pleasure would I get out of watching scantily-clad women gyrating against a pole?"

"I can think of some pleasure." Montgomery snorted a laugh as he poured himself a whiskey.

"Sebastien would never want to go anywhere so coarse." Lady Cordelia sniffed as she took a tall glass of gin and tonic from him.

Sebastien looked at me and Helen. "Would you ladies like anything?"

"Oh, of course! Don't stand on ceremony," Lady Cordelia said, finally noticing us. "You can get your own drinks. Or Monty will fix you drinks if you want one."

"It would be my pleasure. What's your poison?" Montgomery asked. "We've got it all here." He gestured to the full drinks cabinet.

I decided to stick to something soft, and Helen had a glass of champagne.

"We've been showing your new employees around the place," Montgomery said as he handed around the drinks before topping up his own.

Lady Cordelia nodded. "We're short-staffed at the moment. I would have had the butler show you around if he hadn't put his back out. I'm also busy planning a big charity gala, otherwise I'd have done it. I hope the boys haven't been too much of a nuisance."

"They've been very helpful," I said. "I think I can find my way around without getting too lost."

"It is something of a maze," Lady Cordelia said. "But it's home, and you'll get used to it if you stay here long enough."

Flipper and Big Ginge started following Leo around the room, staying a few paces back as he drifted around.

Leo stopped by Lady Cordelia's shoulder, and Flipper joined him and sat by her feet. Big Ginge remained a few steps back.

"Is your dog well behaved?" she asked. "I did have my doubts about letting him come into the castle, given the amount of cats we have here, but I was assured he was trained."

"He's not a problem." I tried to keep my attention on Lady Cordelia, despite the fact Leo was prodding her with a finger and frowning.

She wrapped her arms around herself and shuddered. "Well, he can sit in the corner while we have dinner. I won't have animals begging at the table. Leo always insisted on having a cat on his lap whenever he ate. He'd feed it pieces of food off his plate. It was so unhygienic."

That comment earned her several more prods from Leo. He wasn't happy with his wife. I wondered if it had more to do with her involvement in his death than her comments about the animals.

"Flipper won't do any begging," I said. That wasn't strictly true. He did, but only with people he knew. And he was guaranteed to get a treat off my plate whenever the opportunity arose.

I settled Flipper in the corner, Big Ginge seeming happy to come along as well. I stroked Flipper's head several times to calm him as he kept his gaze on Leo.

"I think he's a nice ghost," I whispered. "Don't go getting yourself worked up that he's in the room with us. He won't do me any harm."

Flipper gave another whine and nudged me with his nose, before sitting down. Big Ginge curled up next to him. Both of them were watching Leo.

Leo was observing the group in the dining room with interest, shaking his head when Montgomery became too loud, but his gaze kept returning to Lady Cordelia.

Perhaps he missed his wife, and was sad he hadn't had an opportunity to say goodbye before he died. I could be making assumptions about his death. This could be the reason he was here, and it had nothing to do with the way he died.

I walked back to Helen's side and turned away so no one could see me talking, pretending to inspect a painting on the wall. "Leo's very interested in Lady

Cordelia. See how she's shivering? It's because Leo keeps prodding her."

"She's got a lot to gain by him being gone." Helen pretended to look at the painting as well. "Having your very own castle must be quite tempting."

I turned back to the group and watched as Lady Cordelia continued to fuss over Sebastien.

He didn't seem to be enjoying it. Although there was a smile on his face, it looked strained, and his eyes were narrowed as Lady Cordelia picked imaginary pieces of fluff from his jacket.

"Someone needs to watch out. Being clingy is not attractive," Helen muttered.

The dining room door opened. A tall, narrow-faced man with a mess of blond hair entered. He was closely followed by a plump blonde woman with brilliant blue eyes and a pouty mouth.

"Darlings! You're just in time for dinner." Lady Cordelia hurried over and kissed them both. I could instantly see the family resemblance. This must be Julius and Tabitha Babington.

"We weren't sure we'd make it, Mommy," Julius said. "Tabitha insisted on stopping off for a drink with some of her awful friends. I only just managed to drag her away in time." His hands fluttered over his chest before he jammed them in his pant pockets.

Tabitha yawned and looked around the room, boredom clear on her pretty face. "I arranged to meet my friends weeks ago. I couldn't let them down. It would have been rude if I hadn't turned up."

"You're both here now. That's the main thing," Lady Cordelia said. "Let's all sit down. The food will be served in a moment."

Helen and I waited until everyone sat in their usual seats, before picking our own chairs. I ended up sitting with Sebastien on my right and Helen on my left. She had the misfortune of being next to Montgomery who was already turning up his flirting abilities and pouring her a large glass of white wine.

"Children, this is Helen Holiday and Lorna Shadow." Lady Cordelia gestured toward us. "They're starting work for the estate. Helen will be our seamstress and Lorna will oversee all of my administration."

Both children barely acknowledged us, Julius managing a brief smile before turning to speak to his sister.

Sebastien leaned toward me. "In case you haven't figured it out, that's Tabitha and Julius Babington. They live here some of the time. Julius considers himself in training to take over the estate at the earliest opportunity."

"What are you whispering about?" Julius glared at Sebastien from the other side of the table.

"I was telling Lorna who you are," Sebastien said. "Since you can't be bothered to tell her yourself."

"She should know who we are," Tabitha said.

"That's no way to welcome our new employees," Sebastien said.

Lady Cordelia sat at the head of the table, and leaned over to pat his hand. "They're being high-spirited, darling. Don't concern yourself with them."

Sebastien's eyes narrowed but he nodded. He leaned back to me. "More like they're being rude. It's their default setting."

"I heard that," Julius said. "Why don't you go and do something useful. What is it you do again for money?"

"Asks Mommy for it." Tabitha tittered a laugh and shoved her napkin over her mouth.

"Now, don't go teasing Sebastien," Lady Cordelia said. "You know he does a lot of work for charity. He's very dedicated to his passions."

"None of which he gets paid for," Julius said. "I'm having work done on the estate soon, you can always join the work crew. I'm thinking of having a new swimming pool installed. We need some extra hands to dig out the hole."

"That won't be necessary," Sebastien said. "Thanks for your generous offer, though."

"I pay above minimum wage." Julius's blue eyes narrowed as he glared at Sebastien. "I'm not sure what your experience is. Have you ever worked before?"

Sebastien thumped a hand on the table. "You know I have."

"There's no point in annoying each other." Lady Cordelia patted Sebastien's hand rapidly, concern on her face. "Let's all get along and have a nice dinner together. No squabbling allowed."

Sebastien huffed under his breath a few times, but didn't say anything else.

The food arrived a moment later, providing a welcome distraction. There was a rich tomato and basil soup with crusty homemade bread to begin with. After the soup bowls were cleared, we all had a generous portion of salmon and balsamic roasted vegetables.

The whole time the meal was being eaten, I was keeping an eye on Leo as he drifted around the table, occasionally pausing to listen to what people had to say, before floating back to Lady Cordelia's chair and resting his hands on the back. I could see he was very interested in his wife, which made me all the more convinced she could be involved with his demise.

"We had a record number of visitors today," Julius said. "I checked the log before coming here."

"It's good that we're so popular," Lady Cordelia said. "It'll mean we can get the new heating system installed before winter sets in."

"It'll take more than a few extra grubby tourists to pay for that," Julius said. "We need to find at least another forty thousand before we sign off on that project."

"The money will come in," Lady Cordelia said. "So far, autumn is proving to be lovely. The sunshine always brings the tourists here in droves. Another few good weekends with lots of visitors, and we'll be able to get the heating done." She rubbed her hands over her arms. "And I feel the need for it tonight. This room seems so cold. I must be sitting in a draft."

I bit my bottom lip. It wasn't a draft causing the problem, but her husband's ghost.

"This doesn't feel like home anymore," Tabitha said. "All those strangers traipsing around, getting in the way."

"They don't come into your private quarters, darling," Lady Cordelia said. "We do have our own rooms we can retreat to when the tourists get too much. And they never see the real castle, not what goes on behind the scenes. You know we need to keep the tourists coming in."

"I have an idea about that." Julius adjusted the collar of his shirt.

"No! I don't want to keep talking about business over dinner," Lady Cordelia said. "This should be family time."

"If it's family time, why are two staff members and your boyfriend sitting at the table?" Tabitha asked.

"Castles don't pay for themselves," Julius said. "And they definitely don't pay for expensive clothes for your toy boy."

"I'm not a toy boy." Sebastien spoke through gritted teeth. "And didn't your mother recently buy you a new car?"

"It was a business expense," Julius said. "I need to look presentable when I go out to meet potential clients. The Babingtons have a reputation to maintain."

"Daddy would never have wanted the castle to turn into this." Tabitha stabbed at a piece of carrot on her plate. "He would be embarrassed to see what was going on. With the castle and with you and your... man friend." She gestured across the table at Sebastien.

Helen kicked me under the table.

I raised my eyebrows in response. This family discussion was getting out of hand.

"Your father would be happy I've found somebody else," Lady Cordelia said. "He wouldn't want me to be on my own. And I do hate to be lonely."

"He wouldn't want you to be with him," Tabitha said. "I should be dating Sebastien, not you."

"I didn't know you cared," Sebastien said.

"I meant, you're more my age," Tabitha said. "I would never want to go out with you. I have no idea what your background is. I doubt it's anything good, though. The first time I met you, you were wearing worn-out leather shoes and a second-hand jacket."

"Children, please! You know I'm fond of Sebastien. He's staying here," Lady Cordelia said. "I want him around. He makes me happy."

"What about our happiness?" Tabitha pouted. "Don't we get a say in what goes on in our own home?"

"If you did, you'd close the doors to the tourists and we would lose everything," Lady Cordelia said.

"Daddy didn't like the tourists coming in and staring at us in our home," Tabitha said.

"Your father didn't care what happened to the castle," Lady Cordelia said. "He only loved his cats."

I looked at Leo, and he gave an shrug and nodded.

"He loved me," Tabitha said.

"Only because you spent so much time with his wretched animals," Lady Cordelia said.

Tabitha stroked a hand down what looked like a suspiciously real fur collar on her fitted black sweater. "That had nothing to do with it. I was his only daughter. Of course he loved me."

Leo gave another shrug and looked down at his hands.

"He wanted an enormous animal sanctuary in the grounds," Julius said. "That's hardly going to make the estate enough money to keep going."

"The sanctuary we have is large enough," Lady Cordelia said. "Anyway, I've made a decision about the cats. I'm looking into getting rid of them."

Leo shot into the air and spun around the table, causing an icy cold draught as he did so.

Flipper jumped to his feet and barked.

Big Ginge's ears flattened against his head and he hissed.

Lady Cordelia glared at me. "I thought your dog was well behaved?"

"Something must have startled him." I gestured at Flipper to lie down. "I'm sorry to hear you won't be helping any more cats, especially since it was your husband's passion."

"His passions have no importance here anymore," Lady Cordelia said. "He spent far too much time and money on those creatures. He should have been focusing on the estate."

"But not filling it with tourists," Tabitha said.

"We need them," Lady Cordelia said. "If it weren't for the visitors we receive every year, we'd have to sell the castle."

"Father was on the right track when it came to animals. The problem was that he was thinking too small," Julius said.

"You want more cats here?" Tabitha shot an incredulous look at her brother.

"Not cats, you imbecile," Julius said. "The damned things make me sneeze. We need big animals. We should turn the grounds into a wildlife park. People pay big money to drive past dangerous animals."

"That's a ridiculous idea," Sebastien said.

"You don't get a say in how the estate is run," Julius said. "Mommy, can't you keep him under control?"

"I'm not a dog," Sebastien said.

"Hah! Actually, you do remind me of one," Tabitha said, her blue eyes narrowing. "The way you chase around after Mommy, begging for handouts all the time."

"He doesn't do that," Lady Cordelia said. "Ignore them, darling." She smiled at Sebastien.

Leo kept spinning around the table, his agitation clear.

I shook my head as I began to get dizzy. He needed to calm down or everyone would be affected.

"All this talk of business is making me bored," Montgomery said. "Why don't we play some after-dinner games?"

"Games are for children," Tabitha said.

"We could play cards for money," Montgomery said.

"I wouldn't mind a game," Julius said.

"How about you, Sebastien?" Montgomery asked.

"I'm leaving." Sebastien pushed back his chair and stood.

Lady Cordelia grabbed his hand and jumped up. "There's no need to leave. Why don't we go for a walk around the grounds?"

"Either he goes or we do," Julius said. "We'd never have come to dinner if we'd known he was going to be here."

"Sebastien will remain as my dinner guest for as long as I wish it." Lady Cordelia's eyes narrowed as she glared at her children. "You will learn to like him."

"So long as you don't go marrying him and we end up having to call him daddy, I really don't mind." Tabitha tittered out another laugh. "Can you imagine that, Sebastien as our stepfather?" She nudged Julius with an elbow.

"We aren't getting married," Sebastien said quietly.

"Well, not yet, darling," Lady Cordelia said. "Maybe one day."

Sebastien looked at Tabitha and then Julius, cold fury clear on his face. "It's time I left."

"Don't let the door hit you on the way out," Julius called.

Sebastien reached the door at the same time as Leo, who was making another dizzying circuit of the room. He shot straight through Sebastian without stopping.

I grimaced. That would feel horrible, like he'd just been dumped in an ice bath and then left to drip dry in a freezer.

Sebastien staggered back several steps, before shaking out his arms and shooting a surprised look over his shoulder.

"Is everything all right, darling?" Lady Cordelia asked. "You've gone very pale."

"I might be coming down with something." Sebastien pressed the back of his hand to his forehead. "I feel... most odd."

Lady Cordelia hurried over and touched his cheek.

Sebastien jerked away as if her touch hurt him.

"Oh! You do feel clammy," she said. "Would you like me to send for the doctor? And you can always stay here if you feel unwell."

"If he's sick then he needs to leave," Tabitha said. "I don't want him infecting me."

"I'll be fine." Sebastien pulled open the door. "I'm already feeling better."

"I'll come with you." Lady Cordelia hurried after him.

"You'll get used to this." Montgomery grinned at me and Helen as he topped up his whiskey before returning to the table. "It's never a good dinner party without a family argument."

"Uncle Monty! Don't be mean," Tabitha said. "You know we don't like Sebastien being here."

"He's not so bad," Montgomery said. "And he keeps your mother happy. If she's happy, it means she's not picking on me. I get to have as much fun as I like while good old Seb keeps her busy."

"Have you had a chance to look over those plans I gave you?" Julius asked.

Montgomery waved a hand in front of his face. "I've not had a chance. It's got something to do with your animal park, hasn't it?"

Leo knocked over three candlesticks on the table, and we all jumped.

Montgomery leaped up and extinguished the candle flames before they could do any damage to the table. "What made them do that?" He tested the weight of one of the candles in his hand.

Flipper gave another bark as Leo continued to bump against the table, making the dishes rattle.

"It could be an earthquake," Julius said. "They happen in this country, but they're usually so weak, most people don't notice them."

"What nonsense. An earthquake in Yorkshire." Tabitha snorted a laugh.

"I'm telling you, it happens," Julius said. "Now, Uncle Monty, about this animal park. It'll be a winning opportunity. There's a lot of initial upfront investment, but once it's open, it will be a goldmine."

Tabitha gave a loud yawn and stretched her arms over her head. "Let's not waste our time talking about the silly animal park. Let's go play Uncle Monty's dumb card games instead."

"The park's a brilliant idea," Julius looked affronted at her comment.

"And my card games are never dumb," Montgomery said.

"Oh, whatever." Tabitha stood and dumped her napkin on the table. "I need something to keep me entertained. Your card games will do. Bring along that bottle of vodka over there. We might as well make it a lively one." She grabbed Julius's elbow and dragged him out of the dining room, still telling him to shut up about the park every time he opened his mouth.

Montgomery walked over to grab a bottle of vodka and an open bottle of champagne. He looked at me and Helen. "You're welcome to join us. Tabitha and Julius are spoiled brats, but they're family, so I let them get away with it. I don't have much choice really. If I get on their bad sides, I might have my allowance cut."

I looked at Leo, who'd stopped spinning around the room. He stood next to the table, his arms folded over his chest and his mouth set in a frown. "We'll pass on the card game. It's been an entertaining enough evening already. I can't handle too much excitement in one night."

"And we should get an early night," Helen said as she faked a yawn. "All this excitement is exhausting."

"You look like a woman who can hold her own." Montgomery grinned at Helen. "I'll get you playing cards with me one night."

"I'm not a gambler," she said.

"Then we can play strip poker." Montgomery winked.

"Good night, Montgomery." Helen stood and turned her back on him.

He laughed as he left the room, the bottles of alcohol in his hands.

"You can calm down now," I said to Leo. "No more spinning around the room like that. It makes me feel sick."

"You weren't the only one," Helen said. "I couldn't see what the ghost was doing, but I could feel it. It felt like I was on board a ship, and I don't have the best sea legs. The salmon I ate at dinner is very unhappy at the moment."

"Mine too," I said. "And Leo upset Flipper and Big Ginge as well."

Leo looked mournfully at the floor.

"I understand you're not happy with the plans your family has, but there's no point in trying to scare them out of the castle."

Leo gave a shrug and then nodded.

"I might be tempted to do just that if they were going to get rid of all of my beloved animals," Helen said, "and replace them with hippos, or whatever it is Julius wants to do. It's so unfair that Lady Cordelia is closing the sanctuary."

Leo rattled the table and nodded again.

"I agree. But at least this evening has been useful," I said. "We have a whole load of new suspects who'd benefit from Leo's death. We just need to figure out which one killed him and made it look like an accident."

Chapter 7

Despite sharing my bed with not only Flipper but also Big Ginge, I'd had a good night of sleep, and awoke convinced that Leo needed help. Even if it was just to help him figure out how he really died, I'd be there for him.

Murder or not, I got the impression he wasn't going to leave this castle until he knew what happened to him. And that meant he wouldn't leave me alone until we'd resolved this mystery.

The more I found out about Leo and his family, the more I realized there were plenty of people who would benefit from his death. Murder was looking ever more likely.

I showered, and dressed in a smart black suit, before going to the kitchen with Flipper, Big Ginge following closely behind us.

Before we got to the kitchen, the cat made a detour out of a flap in a door and vanished.

Helen was already sitting at the kitchen table when we arrived. Daphne was also in the kitchen, pouring boiling water into a teapot.

"Good morning," Daphne said brightly. "I hope you enjoyed your first day in the castle."

"Dinner was interesting," I said as I sat next to Helen.

"Helen was just telling me all about it," Daphne said.

"I was at the part where Julius told Sebastien he was a greedy toy boy," Helen said.

"And, let me guess, they had a big argument after that?" Daphne set the teapot on the table and handed me a white mug.

"That's right," I said. "Does that often happen around here?"

"It does. It's the children who are the problem." Daphne leaned on the back of a chair. "They've got lots of half thought-out ideas about what they want to do with the castle, and don't consider anybody else. It's not my place to say, but I think that since Leo died, they've been allowed to run wild. They both have their own places in London, all paid for by Lady Cordelia, plus they've been given their own car. And neither of them works. Well, Tabitha goes into some little fashion magazine a couple of days a week, but I don't think she gets a salary. And Julius struts around the estate make-believing he owns the castle. They run Lady Cordelia ragged. She's struggling to hold things together."

"Do you think Lady Cordelia misses Leo?" I asked.

Daphne scrubbed the end of her nose. "They were fond of each other, but it wasn't the sort of love that set the sheets on fire every night. To begin with, I don't think the age difference was an issue, but the older Leo got the more eccentric he became. It irritated Lady Cordelia that he spent so much time on his passions."

"You mean the cats?" I asked.

"He did love his animals," Daphne said. "Have you been over to the animal sanctuary yet?"

"Not yet," I said. "We might get a chance later after we've finished work."

"Leo spared no expense on those cats. I think that was one of the things that irritated Lady Cordelia so much. He was happy to spend thousands on a new indoor heating system for the cats, but didn't want to upgrade the system in the castle, so the family shivered in winter."

The kitchen door slammed open and two women dashed in, both wearing matching black pants and jackets. One held a hanky to her nose and the other's cheeks were bright red, her eyes full of tears.

"Sandy! Nell! What's the matter?" Daphne bustled over to them, concern on her face.

"That dreadful woman is threatening to shut down the sanctuary." The taller of the two women blew her nose into the hanky. "She's got such a cold heart. How can she throw those angels out? She's hateful."

"Sandy, that's no way to talk about Lady Cordelia." Daphne flapped her hands at the woman. "Come sit at the table both of you and calm yourselves before you say something you'll regret." She ushered them in front of her, and they both took seats.

The women eyed me and Helen and then looked at Daphne.

"You won't have met Lady Cordelia's new employees. This is Lorna Shadow and Helen Holiday." Daphne made the introductions.

"Poor you. I'm sorry you're having to work for such an awful woman," Sandy said.

"What were you saying about her closing the sanctuary?" I asked.

"She hates cats." Nell pushed her dark blonde messy curls off her face and scrubbed her eyes. "And she was jealous of the amount of time Leo spent at the sanctuary."

"We were just talking about that." Daphne passed around more mugs and filled them with strong tea. She put two sugar cubes in Nell and Sandy's mugs.

"She can't get rid of the sanctuary." Sandy thumped a hand on the table. "Where will all the cats go?"

"And Leo would be dead against it if he was still here," Nell said. "He always talked about having a permanent place for unwanted cats to live. He was adamant about that. Now he's gone, Lady Cordelia can do what she likes. And I know Julius has been sniffing around as well, talking about having wild animals running loose in the estate. It's madness."

"With a bit of luck, one of the lions will eat him if he makes it happen," Sandy said. "That'll serve him right."

The kitchen door was shoved open again. This time, Big Ginge strolled in, his tail raising as he saw us all sitting around the table.

"And here's one of Leo's favorites." Nell jumped up and grabbed Big Ginge. "The two of them were inseparable. They went everywhere together. This little sweetie used to sit and watch for Leo to come to the sanctuary and would follow him around, double checking everything was under control with the other cats, just like he owned the place. A real little lord of manor."

"Lady Cordelia hates the cats even more now," Sandy said. "Since one of them smothered Leo in his sleep."

Big Ginge struggled out of Nell's grip and hopped to the ground, before strolling over and sniffing noses with Flipper, who wagged his tail at his new friend.

"Is that what you think happened?" I asked Sandy.

"Not for a second," Sandy said with a disgruntled snort. "I'm sure something fishy is going on over the way Leo died. It was all kept quiet because the family didn't want a scandal."

"They think it'll affect the bottom line if tourists know someone was killed here," Nell said.

"You think Leo was killed?" Helen's eyebrows shot up.

"What nonsense," Daphne said. "It was a horrible accident that's all. Don't go putting daft ideas into these girls' heads. They might decide to leave if they think the family are skulking around the corridors at night with dark intentions."

Nell shrugged. "Lady Cordelia can do what she likes now Leo's gone. I bet she did snuff him out. By killing Leo she removed the barrier that stopped her from getting rid of the cats."

"And once they're gone, we're out of work," Sandy said. "We've lived on the estate for five years. I'd hate to leave. It would break my heart worrying about what would happen to the cats. I expect Lady Cordelia will throw them in the lake."

Helen gasped. "Really?"

"No! Of course not. Stop all this nasty talk," Daphne said. "Lady Cordelia isn't that bad. She may have ideas that are different from her late husband's but that doesn't make her an evil person. You know things need to change if they're going to keep the castle running. Have you seen the east wing? There's damp on the walls and a hole in the roof that needs fixing."

"Change something other than the sanctuary," Nell said. "Open up more of the inside of the castle. Tourists would get a thrill if they saw the family sleeping in their fancy four-poster beds at night. They could even have peep shows when they're in the shower. That would draw the crowds if they got a chance to see how posh people take a wash."

"Now you're just being silly." Daphne flapped a dishcloth at Nell. "I don't agree with getting rid of the cats, but perhaps we can have wild animals and cats in the grounds. That way, everyone is happy."

"I bet Lady Cordelia won't like that idea." Sandy snuffled in her hanky before drinking some tea.

"And Julius is the one obsessed with having the wild animals stalking around," Nell said. "He thinks the cats are a waste of money because they don't bring in a, what did he call it when he was explaining his stupid vision the other week, a good return on investment. As if you think about things like that when you're looking after unwanted animals. The man has no heart. Just like his mother."

"And Leo had too much heart." Daphne gave a sigh. "He was too soft with the animals and the people who worked with them." She gave Sandy and Nell a stern look. "Things are changing and we all have to get used to that. It's been almost a year since Leo died. We knew plans were afoot to alter things around here."

"Maybe Lady Cordelia is hoping we'll leave first and save her the trouble of firing us," Nell said. "Every time she visits the sanctuary, she always finds something to complain about. She's just looking for a reason to get rid of it all."

"Then make sure you do your jobs properly and she won't have any cause for complaint," Daphne said.

"Do you mind if we drop by the sanctuary at some point?" I asked Sandy and Nell. "I love animals. It would be great to meet the cats."

"You'd be welcome any time," Sandy said, smiling brightly at me. "It's always a joy to meet another animal lover. We're there every day. If neither of us is around, feel free to look about. The cats always like visitors."

"You'd better hurry if you want to see the sanctuary," Nell said, a scowl making her blue eyes pinch at the corners. "Otherwise, all the cats will be gone, all thanks to Lady Cordelia."

Sandy downed her tea and stood. She looked at Nell. "Come on, we'd better get back. The cats need feeding and their litter cleaned out. There's always so much work to be done."

Nell tried to stroke Big Ginge, but he skipped around the kitchen just out of her reach. "Cats are much better company than people, anyway."

"I'm sure you don't include us in that," Daphne said.

"You're all right, I suppose." Nell stomped out the kitchen, closely followed by Sandy.

"Welcome to the world of crazy cat ladies," Daphne said. "Those two are so dedicated to their work, I'm surprised they don't grow whiskers and tails of their own. I'm sure they'd be happier being cats than humans."

That didn't sound like a terrible swap to me. Cats got to spend most of their time sleeping, eating or exploring. Not a bad life if you could get it.

"They were right about Leo spending all his spare time at the sanctuary," Daphne said. "I do hope Lady Cordelia has a change of heart and doesn't shut it down. I'm not sure those two are suitable for working anywhere else. Leo spoiled them and gave then free rein with the cats. Now he's not here to look out for the sanctuary or Sandy and Nell."

"We need to see this sanctuary for ourselves," I said. "It sounds impressive."

"If you're into cats, it's the place to go." Daphne walked to the kitchen counter and arranged muffins on a plate. "Help yourselves. These are fresh out of the oven."

"Thanks." I took two warm blueberry muffins and gestured Helen to follow me out of the kitchen. We had suspects to discuss, and I didn't want to be overheard.

Helen grabbed her own muffins, and after a quick goodbye to Daphne, we left the kitchen, Flipper hot on my heels in the hope of getting some muffin of his own.

"Sandy and Nell don't think much of the family." Helen bit into her blueberry muffin. "Lady Cordelia and Julius are on the top of their hate list."

"I've been thinking that Lady Cordelia might be the main suspect in Leo's death, but with Julius hating the way the castle is run and having his eye on changing things, we need to consider him a serious contender."

"And Tabitha as well," Helen said.

"What did she do to make you think she could be involved?"

"She was mean to us," Helen said.

I arched an eyebrow. "Which makes her a killer?"

"Which makes her not a nice person."

"She was also pretty mean to Sebastien," I said. "Okay, we may as well consider all possibilities."

"And what about Sebastien? A younger lover with no money arrives on the scene at just the right time. Did he see an opportunity and decide to get rid of Leo so he could snag some cash?"

"I wonder how long he's been around. Perhaps Lady Cordelia met him before Leo died." I shook my head. "Sebastien doesn't strike me as a money-grubber, though."

"I don't think he's here for love," Helen said. "He was getting annoyed with Lady Cordelia for fussing over him last night. She's trying to shape him into her perfect boy toy by buying him gifts and clothes and showing him off to her friends. That must be humiliating for him."

"Sebastien can go on the bottom of the list for now," I said.

"And then there's Montgomery," Helen said. "A charming drunken younger brother who squanders all his money."

I ate my sweet blueberry muffin as I considered the growing list of suspects. "Let's focus on Lady Cordelia first. I'll see if I can find out anything useful when we're working together today."

"You think she has her world domination plan tucked away in a filing cabinet?"

"It would be handy if she did," I said. "But I'm more interested in anything she has to say about Leo. She didn't appear sad about his death when I mentioned it the first time we met, and she does have an awful lot to gain by him no longer being alive. Maybe she got tired of having a much older husband who loved animals more than her. Then she met Sebastien, saw a chance to be wealthy and take a younger lover, and decided to do something about it."

"There's taking charge of your life and then there's being a selfish animal hater who kills her husband," Helen said.

I finished my second muffin, feeding Flipper the last bite much to his delight. "Let's meet later at the cat sanctuary. I'll let you know what I find out."

"Good luck." Helen gave me a quick thumbs up as we parted ways.

I headed to Lady Cordelia's study to start my first day of work. The door was already open when I got there.

As I entered, I saw a wall covered with books, a large desk set by a bay window, and an enormous stone fireplace dominating one end of the room.

Lady Cordelia sat behind the desk. She had a pair of glasses perched on the end of her nose, and her hair was clipped off her face as she studied a document in front of her.

She glanced up from her paperwork and gestured to a seat on the opposite side of the desk. "Good morning, Lorna. I hope you're settling in well."

"Yes, I am. All good so far." I sat in the chair. "Thank you for dinner last night."

Lady Cordelia peered at me in silence for several seconds. "Yes, dinner was an... event. And we didn't get a chance to talk about your duties. My family can be feisty at times. They rather took my attention from my plan to chat with you and Helen."

I nodded. "Sometimes, you have the worst fights with the people you love the most."

"I didn't realize I'd employed a philosopher as well as a personal assistant." A small smile played on Lady Cordelia's lips. "But that is very true of this family. It won't happen again. And I have a specific task for you to focus on in your first few weeks here."

"What's that?" I expected to be given the usual task of re-organizing the filing system, typing dictation, or sending out letters.

"You're to dispose of the cats in the animal sanctuary."

I blinked at Lady Cordelia and swallowed, not liking where this conversation was going. "I'm not sure what you mean."

"Leo's wretched cat sanctuary needs to go." She smacked a hand on the desk. "We need to change things on the estate. The cats are a burden we can do without. Do you know how much it costs to run the sanctuary?"

I shook my head. "An animal sanctuary will never make you any money. Didn't your late husband like animals and want to help them? He wouldn't have set it up to make money."

"He did adore animals, but as you rightly pointed out, he's my late husband. He doesn't get a say in how this estate is run anymore." Lady Cordelia's top lip curled. "And I want those cats gone. It costs us almost one hundred thousand a year to feed them and pay the staff bills. They have indoor heated rooms! They're animals for goodness sake. They don't need heaters, they have fur."

"Perhaps you can buy cheaper cat litter or only heat their rooms some of the time to cut down on costs."

"There's no point in trying to reduce the costs at the sanctuary," Lady Cordelia said. "The best thing to do is get rid of them. It'll leave the way clear to expand and develop the estate without those mangy animals getting in the way."

Any feelings of goodwill I had toward Lady Cordelia vanished, and I narrowed my eyes. "And you want me to oversee getting rid of them?"

"I know it's not typical work for a personal assistant, but we need all hands on deck," Lady Cordelia said. "Having looked at your resume and taken up your references, I know you're a woman who can turn her hand to anything. Do this for me, and I'll consider raising your salary when you're successful."

I blinked several times, processing the information, a sinking feeling in my stomach. "What do you suggest I do with the cats?"

"Do what you like with them." Lady Cordelia shrugged her narrow shoulders. "Probably putting them to sleep is the best thing. No one else will want them."

"You want me to have the cats killed?" My hands clenched in my lap.

"Or whatever you like," Lady Cordelia said. "Get them out of my way and do it quickly. The sooner they're gone the better. Consider this a test of your abilities. It will show me how adaptable you are."

"I need time to consider this. Relocating fifty animals doesn't happen overnight."

"I want you to make it happen, and don't take long about it. Having those cats everywhere is a reminder of Leo and what he used to spend his time on." Lady Cordelia let out a sigh as she removed her glasses and cleaned the lenses. "Lorna, do you believe in reincarnation?"

"I'm not sure," I said. Would a ghost be considered a form of reincarnation? "Why do you ask?"

"Because if such a thing exists, I know for sure that Leo would have come back as a cat. For all I know, he might be one of the new intakes at the sanctuary, stalking around and seeing what the rest of us are doing." Lady Cordelia laughed bitterly. "And I know, if he could have done, he'd have married a cat."

I bit my bottom lip. "I don't think that's legal."

She placed her glasses down. "Yes, well, just deal with the cats. That's your first and only task for now. I hope you won't let me down. Your future here depends on it."

I could hardly refuse my new employer the first task she'd given me, despite the thought of having to send those cats away to goodness knows where making me feel sick. "I'll look into it right away."

Lady Cordelia stood and strode out from behind her desk. "You may use whatever resources are in here, and you have your own laptop over on that desk." She pointed behind me to a small desk in the corner of the room. "Get to work on dealing with the cats first. We'll sort out the rest of your duties at a later date." She left the room and closed the door behind her.

I looked at Flipper, my stomach churning with a mixture of shock and horror.

Lady Cordelia was definitely on the top of my suspect list now.

Chapter 8

I spent the morning researching local animal sanctuaries, thinking I'd be able to relocate the cats to other places that loved animals as much as Leo had. I had a list of contacts to call, but felt in need of a break before I started. And since I was in charge of getting rid of the sanctuary, I needed to see it for myself and assess how big this challenge would be.

The sun was still warm as I walked into the grounds, Flipper by my side, his nose in the air as he caught an interesting smell. So far, autumn seemed to be holding off, despite the hints of orange and brown in the trees.

I spotted a sign saying *Paws and Purrs Sanctuary*, and headed along the path toward it.

Flipper increased his pace and his ears shot up.

"You go steady with these cats," I said. "Some of them won't like you, and you don't want to scare them."

Flipper gave me a look as if to say *would I?* He slowed his pace and remained by my side.

We reached a small wooden office. I knocked on the door before walking in.

Sandy was seated behind a desk. Three cats sat on top of it. They all paused in their grooming activities and regarded me with large intelligent eyes.

"I hope you don't mind me dropping by," I said to Sandy, instantly feeling guilty at knowing what I was going to have to do to the sanctuary.

Sandy stood from her seat and smiled. "You're welcome. Do you want to hang out with some cool cats?"

"If you've got the time to show me around that would be great," I said. "And Flipper wouldn't mind tagging along as well. He loves cats."

"So long as he behaves himself, he's welcome." Sandy scooped a large white cat off the desk and settled him in her arms. "This one's called Stevie."

"You name all your cats?" I tickled Stevie behind his ears.

"Every single one." Pride resonated through Sandy's voice. "Some of them come to us with names, but others, we have no clue about their background. We pick a name that suits their personality."

Stevie purred loudly and pressed against my hand.

"I'll show you the animal homes." Sandy pulled open the door, and I followed her out with Flipper. "We don't like to call them cages. And they're top of the range, with all the toys and luxuries a cat could dream of. Some of the cats have had such a bad time of it, they deserve to be pampered."

It was like Sandy was deliberately trying to make me feel even guiltier for being the tyrant who'd be throwing out these poor abused babies. I had to find a way to change Lady Cordelia's mind about closing the sanctuary.

We walked along a neat gravel pathway, and I could hear cats meowing as we drew nearer.

"We have ten cat homes per row." Sandy pointed at the large, metal cages. "They have an indoor section where they can sleep or get away from prying eyes if they want a bit of privacy. They also all have their own outdoor runs. Each cat is separated if they didn't come in with a sibling or a friend, so there's no problems with fighting or any of them sneakily getting together and breeding. We neuter and spay the cats when they arrive if it hasn't already been done. Kittens are so cute, but they need a lot of looking after."

Flipper poked his nose at one of the cat houses. A large black paw appeared and swiped at him. He backed up swiftly and gave me a worried glance.

Sandy laughed. "That's Panther. He lives up to his name. He's the biggest black cat I've ever seen, with a temper to match."

I peered cautiously into the cage, and was met by a pair of unblinking green eyes. "He's beautiful, if a little scary."

"We've had him a long time," Sandy said. "Most of the cats here have what I call special needs. Some have behavioral problems or have been so badly treated they don't trust people anymore. I can't say I blame them when you hear some of the horror stories about what people do to their animals."

I ruffled Flipper's fur as I recalled our first meeting. He'd been dumped on the side of the road as a puppy. "People can be so thoughtless."

"At least we're here to show them that there's some good in the world," Sandy said.

I nodded, guilt running through me like acid. I would find these cats amazing new homes, even if it killed me.

She led me along the rest of the pens, introducing me to all the cats and giving me information on their backgrounds. It was such a great setup. I could understand why Leo was so passionate about helping these animals.

"When I think about what Lady Cordelia wants to do to the sanctuary, it makes me sick." Sandy walked me and Flipper back to the office, Stevie now asleep in her arms. "She wasn't always like this, though."

"What made her change?" I asked.

"Ever since Sebastien came on the scene, she's been different. Until then, Lady Cordelia was content to let Leo get on with his work helping the cats. She didn't like it, but I think it gave her the chance to have some time on her own."

"Did she meet Sebastien before Leo died?"

Sandy deposited a sleeping Stevie on the desk. "I wouldn't know. He certainly showed up quickly enough after Leo died."

"And Sebastien's making Lady Cordelia get rid of the animals?" I didn't think he'd shown any dislike toward the cats when we were looking around the castle. He certainly hadn't complained about Flipper and Big Ginge when they were in the dining room.

"I don't know much about him," Sandy said. "He seems too young for Lady Cordelia. I can see why he's interested in her, though. She's a recent widow with a heap of money and a castle. I guess a man can overlook a few years if he can get his hands on some of that cash."

"I've met Sebastien. He seems like a nice guy. Not the sort to use a woman because she's wealthy."

"I didn't say he wasn't nice. But nice guys can't live on fresh air." She bent and stroked the back of a skinny tortoiseshell cat who emerged from behind the desk.

"The sanctuary's great," I said. It was time to come clean. "And I hate to have to tell you this, but Lady Cordelia has put me in charge of making sure it closes."

Sandy's green eyes narrowed. "So you're here sneaking around to find out how the place is run. Are you trying to see what we're doing wrong so you have good reason to shut it down?"

I held my hands up as I shook my head. "Absolutely not. The sanctuary is an amazing place. I'm not happy she's put me in charge of closing it."

"So, stop her from doing it. Tell her she's wrong and you can see how important this place is."

"She won't listen to me. Her mind's made up. But I'll do what I can to slow things down," I said. "Perhaps you could get Lady Cordelia out here and show her all the great things you do. That might make her think differently about the place."

"She won't be interested," Sandy said. "The few times she has been out here since Leo died, all she's done is complain. She loathes this place. Giving her a fancy tour and covering her in adorable kittens to get her excited about the unloved cats won't work. Besides, she wouldn't want to mess up her designer shoes by tramping around in the mud."

"I promise you, I'm on your side," I said. "If we can find any way to keep the sanctuary going, I'll make sure it happens. And if I can't, at least between us we can ensure the animals go to safe places. I've already got a list of local rescue centers that could take them in."

Sandy folded her arms over her chest and gave a huff. "It's not right her making you do this. If she wants to get rid of these lovely animals, she should do it herself. She should look each cat in the eye and see just how mean she's being."

"I think it's best if Lady Cordelia's not directly involved. She did mention putting them to sleep."

Sandy gave a strangled cry. "I won't let her near them if she thinks that's going to happen."

"Neither will I. I'll keep you informed as to what's going on. You won't come here one morning and find all the cats gone."

"Well, I should be grateful for small things," Sandy said. "When I tell Nell, she'll be furious. She's more obsessed with the cats than I am. She hates the idea that Lady Cordelia is going to change things."

"Tell her gently. And perhaps the two of you can take some of the cats home with you when you have to go."

"That's another problem we've got to figure out," Sandy said. "We both live on site. The jobs come with accommodation. Not only are we going to have no work, we're going to be out of our homes."

I shook my head, wishing I could say something to reassure Sandy. "I'll do what I can to help." My phone rang and I gave Sandy a quick wave goodbye, before answering it. I smiled as I recognized the number.

"How's your first day at work going?" Zach asked.

"I'm surrounded by cats." I walked a few steps away from the sanctuary.

"Cats?"

"That's right. Flipper's in his element," I said. "He's trying to make friends with every cat he meets. They don't seem too sure about him, though."

"And dare I ask about the castle's other residents?" Caution threaded through Zach's words.

"I've only seen one ghost," I said. "Actually, I'm quite disappointed about that. I expected to be walking into them every time I turned a corner. It seems the castle isn't as full of ghosts as the website claims."

"That's a relief," he said. "I was thinking you'd be surrounded by unhappy ghosts demanding your attention. One ghost is okay."

"I can handle this one. In fact, he seems like a nice old man. He's not caused me any problems." I paused. Zach wouldn't like me revealing this next bit of news. "I don't think he died of natural causes."

I heard him exhale down the phone. "You think he was murdered?"

"It looks like it."

"Do I need to warn you to be careful?"

"I'll do the best I can," I said.

"That's all I ask of you," Zach said. "If you get into trouble, let me know."

"And you'll come help me with your ghost hunting skills?"

He snorted. "I'm not a ghost hunter, but I like to make sure you're safe."

"Okay. You're my gardening knight in shining armor."

"That compliment I will accept."

I grinned. I loved having Zach as my protector. I'd held back from accepting his help in the past, but it didn't feel right when he wasn't around. I liked to know I had him to rely on, no matter how spooky and weird the situation became.

"I was also calling because I've seen details of a house that looks good. Plenty of bedrooms, it needs a bit of work, but it's well within our budget," he said.

"I like the sound of that. Fix up a time and we'll go and see it."

"How about tomorrow evening?"

"It's a date," I said. "Shall I bring Helen?"

"Maybe not," Zach said. "Let's have a look just the two of us to begin with. If we think it's got possibilities, we can get Gunner and Helen along for a second viewing. I'm not sure I can take any more of their bickering right now."

I laughed. "I've mentioned the bickering to Helen. I'm not sure it's going to calm her down, though. She's determined to prove me wrong and show she's not interested in Gunner."

Zach sighed down the phone again. "I'll look forward to their next round of bickering then. I'll send you the details of the house so you can have a look and see what you think."

We'd just said our goodbyes, and I'd turned back toward the house, when the air around me chilled and a wave of dizziness ran through me.

"Leo?" I clutched my arms around my stomach, my vision going blurry. Where was Flipper? I'd been so busy chatting to Zach that I hadn't noticed him disappear.

The air got even colder and my teeth began to chatter. "Leo, stop messing about. I know you're here."

In the distance, I heard Flipper bark and a spitting hiss from a cat. I spun around and saw him facing off with an angry tabby and white cat.

"Flipper! I could do with some help here." My words croaked out of me as my bones chilled.

In front of me, a haze spread across the ground. I staggered backward as the figure of a lady in a long blue gown appeared. Her eye sockets were hollow and her mouth opened in a silent scream.

My hand went to my own mouth as the ghostly lady shimmered in front of me and raised an arm.

Flipper barked again, but it sounded far away this time. What was taking him so long?

Leo suddenly popped into view. He caught hold of the other ghost, and they both vanished as I sank to the ground in a frozen heap.

Chapter 9

I let out a shaky sigh as the temperature returned to normal. I got the impression the blue lady wasn't a benevolent ghost.

Flipper dashed to my side and away from the cat he'd been trying to make friends with. He gave me what I thought was an apologetic look as he circled the spot where the two ghosts had been.

Leo reappeared in front of me and gave a bow.

"Thanks for helping with the other ghost," I said.

He nodded and looked at Flipper who was now circling him.

"Don't worry. Leo is our friend," I said to Flipper. Now Leo had arrived, I was already feeling better. It was that initial energy sapping arrival of a ghost that always got me. Especially when that ghost didn't look like she wanted to make friends.

Leo nodded and patted the top of Flipper's head.

"I've been spending time with your lovely cats." I shook the chill off, stood slowly, and gently strolled toward the castle as I worked feeling back into my fingers and toes.

Leo smiled and looked over his shoulder at the sanctuary.

"I've also been trying to find out who could have killed you. If you're convinced it wasn't a cat, we have a few suspects we need to look into."

Leo drifted along beside me as a cool breeze slipped through the garden. He pointed at his ring finger.

"You think it was Lady Cordelia?" I said. "Do you remember seeing her before you died?"

He shook his head and then looked around the garden. He disappeared, returning a few seconds later with a yellow daisy in his hand.

"Is this for me?" I took the flower quickly, knowing how strange it would appear to anyone who was watching and saw a flower bobbing along next to me.

Leo shook his head, took the flower back and held it to his nose.

I grabbed the flower again. "You smelt flowers just before you died?"

Leo tilted his head from side to side.

"Not flowers, but something floral. A woman's perfume?"

He nodded.

That was another black mark against Lady Cordelia. You didn't get many men who smelled of flowers. "I've discovered that your wife wasn't happy with all the time and money you spent on the cats."

Leo gave a shrug.

"Was she unhappy enough to do something about that?"

I got another shrug in response to that question.

"What about Tabitha?" I asked. "If you're sure it was a woman who killed you, she may have been wearing the perfume that you smelled. Did you have a falling out with her before you died?"

Leo shook his head and gestured at the flower again.

The sound of two women arguing drifted toward me. I increased my speed and rounded the corner of the castle to find Lady Cordelia and Nell glaring at each other. I ducked behind a bush, Flipper following me.

"You're no longer welcome here." Lady Cordelia jabbed her finger at Nell.

Nell's cheeks paled as she took a step closer to Lady Cordelia. "You have no right to get rid of me. Leo wanted me here. He knew how much I love those animals."

"You're as crazy as him," Lady Cordelia said. "And it's time all of you went. I want you gone, and I want the cats gone too."

"You can't get rid of them," Nell yelled. "Leo won't allow it."

"Fortunately for me, Leo is dead," Lady Cordelia said. "Which means I can do whatever I like to the cats. They're on my estate. As are you."

"This was Leo's estate," Nell said. "You probably married him so you could get your hands on all of this. You should respect his wishes."

"What do you know of Leo's wishes?" Lady Cordelia folded her arms over her chest and raised her chin.

"Even though he's no longer here, you know he adored those cats," Nell said. "He would never want them gone. You're dishonoring his memory by even thinking about getting rid of them."

"I don't care what you think about my late husband or those animals," Lady Cordelia said. "I want you to leave this estate. You're no longer employed here."

"You can't make me leave." Nell stamped her foot. "I won't abandon the cats."

"I'll call the police if you don't leave immediately."

Flipper spotted another cat skulking across the grass. He ran out from behind the bush before I could stop him.

Lady Cordelia glanced over and saw me. Her lips pinched together as she moved away from Nell. "This conversation is over."

I took a deep breath as I approached Lady Cordelia, sensing the anger radiating off her. "I didn't mean to listen in. I heard you arguing and came to make sure everything was okay."

"Everything is not okay." Lady Cordelia looked back at Nell, who hadn't moved. "I am sorry you had to see that. Nell has always been a difficult employee. I would have let her go a long time ago, but Leo was stubborn and insisted she stayed. He called her a cat whisperer. He claimed she could bring around the most timid of cats."

"I only met Nell this morning. She seems very into her animals."

"She does have that in common with my late husband," Lady Cordelia said. "If anything, she's worse with the cats than Leo used to be. Nell will calm down. She always gets angry and starts shouting before she's had a chance to think."

"This isn't the first time you've argued?"

Lady Cordelia smiled wryly. "No, and I've seen her like this before. It's time for her to move on, though. I have no hard feelings against Nell, and I want to give her time to get herself sorted and find somewhere new to live, but I can only be so generous. I have to think about the bigger picture and the long term stability of this castle."

"You never know, Nell might take some of the cats with her when she goes," I said. "That will help you out."

"I'll be glad if she does. And I know she'll need the company. No man will ever want Nell and her cat obsession." Lady Cordelia tapped her manicured nails on her thigh as she stared at Nell. "Although, I did wonder..."

"What did you wonder?"

"Well, Leo and Nell were close. They always had their heads together, discussing the cats." Lady Cordelia laughed. "It's silly really. I wondered if they were closer than they should be."

My eyebrows shot up. "You think Nell had a relationship with Leo?"

"Not really," she said. "Maybe I was just jealous that they were both so passionate about the same thing. It's been a while since I've felt such passion."

"Sebastien seems nice," I said. "You must be able to share things with him."

Lady Cordelia looked over at me. "I do, but it's different. Anyway, how are you getting on with removing the cats?"

"I went to the sanctuary. The setup there is great. Is there no way you can keep it?"

"It's out of the question," she said, her gaze hardening. "Just get a move on with whatever it is you have planned. I don't want any more flea bags running around in my castle."

"I'm working on it."

"I want to see results in the next two weeks," Lady Cordelia said. "If you haven't figured out where those cats are going by then, I'll put my own plans into action. And Sandy and Crazy Nell won't like that." She strode away across the gravel toward the main entrance of the castle, ignoring Nell as she did so.

My heart felt heavy as Lady Cordelia left. This was definitely not in the job description I'd read. I couldn't help but feel peeved at being given such a thankless task. Whatever I did, someone would be unhappy. If I annoyed Lady Cordelia too badly she might decide I wasn't suitable for this job and I'd find myself out of work. And, if I closed the sanctuary, Nell and Sandy, and all the cats, would be heartbroken.

I called Flipper away from his pursuit of another cat, before turning and almost walking into Montgomery.

"Ha! I caught you listening into Lady Cordelia's little spat." He lounged against the castle wall, dressed in crumpled linen pants and a matching green jacket.

"Not deliberately," I said. "It was hard not to listen, given how loud they were being." I glanced over my shoulder and saw Nell storming off.

"Cordelia's always arguing with somebody," Montgomery said. "She's never happy unless she's making somebody else miserable."

"Does that include you?"

"Most of the time." He grinned at me. "Fancy a drink? I'll tell you all about my sad little life."

I wasn't much of a drinker, but having just spent a stressful afternoon trying to help fifty unloved cats, a drink sounded like a good idea.

"Why not," I said. "Lead the way."

Montgomery was on the suspect list. Now was as good a time as any to see what he knew about what had happened to Leo.

Chapter 10

Montgomery held his arm out, and I took it as we made our way inside the castle. "Let me show you one of the many fun secrets about this place," he said.

"I'm intrigued. What's the secret?"

"This way." He pulled aside a tapestry in the main hallway.

I stared at the wall. "Nice brickwork."

He laughed before sliding a hand into a space in the bricks. A hidden doorway appeared in front of us.

"Oh! Wow! That is impressive." I peered into the dark corridor that had emerged as he pulled back the door.

"Let's go." As Montgomery stepped forward, a light came on over his head.

Despite the light, the place had an eerie vibe to it. "Where are you taking me?" I stared at one of the denser patches of shadow.

Flipper pressed against my leg and whined.

"Nowhere bad," Montgomery said. "Don't tell me you're afraid of a few cobwebs?"

"No, but we'd better not be going back to that torture room."

Montgomery chuckled. "Oh no. I save the torture room for a special occasion."

"Like a romantic third date?"

He grinned. "Women can't seem to get enough of all that blood and torture stuff."

I shot him a sharp glance out of the corner of my eye, and he laughed again.

"This doesn't look part of the public route around the castle." I brushed a cobweb aside with my hand.

"You'd be right. This castle comes with its own set of secret corridors. They were created when the monasteries were dissolved under Henry VIII and the priests needed somewhere to hide if they wanted to stay alive. There are all sorts of secret corridors and priest holes in here. This corridor runs parallel to the main hallway in the castle. It comes out in the games room."

I shivered in excitement at the thought of being able to creep around the castle with no one knowing where I was. There could be dozens of wide-eyed tourists standing on the other side of the wall. They'd never know we were there.

Montgomery stopped and pressed his hand against the wall. I heard a click and a crack of light appeared in front of us. "It's pretty nifty, isn't it?"

I nodded as he pushed the door open to reveal the games room.

Montgomery led me and Flipper into the room, which was full of comfortable chairs, a large drinks cabinet, several games consoles, and an enormous pool table. "Will you join me for a martini?"

"That sounds good." I did a quick circuit of the room, inhaling old cigar smoke and a hint of whiskey as I did so.

"Take a seat." Montgomery walked to the drinks cabinet and began to mix the martinis. "I find martinis make the world a happier place. They give everything a pretty glow when you've downed a few. I hope you're not finding working with Lady Cordelia too much of an ordeal."

"My first day wasn't so bad." I sat on a brown leather sofa, and Flipper settled by my feet. "But she is insisting I help her get rid of the cat sanctuary. I hadn't planned on leaving my mark on this place by doing that."

Montgomery shook his head as he carried the drinks over and sat next to me. "She does enjoy puncturing people's happiness. My brother loved those cats. I guess that's why she wants to get rid of them."

I took the martini glass and took a sip. It made my eyes water it was so strong. No wonder his world got fuzzy after drinking a couple of these. "Do you think she's doing it out of spite? Getting rid of something Leo loved because she was unhappy with him?"

"She could be." Montgomery leaned back and draped his arm along the sofa. "I try not to get involved in castle politics, though. Being the younger brother, it means I don't have any responsibilities. I was never expected to do anything. Whereas Leo always loved that kind of thing. He enjoyed organizing and making plans for the future. So long as he gave me a bit of money now and again, I was happy to play along and agree with whatever he wanted. And I enjoyed getting to hang out here. As you can see, the castle is a lot of fun."

"You must miss him," I said. "Was Leo your only brother?"

He nodded and the glitter of amusement in his eyes faded. "It was just the two of us. Leo always wanted to be in charge of the castle. He didn't even try to teach me the ropes in preparation for his retirement. He planned to bring in an estate manager when he took a step back."

"You weren't the tiniest bit jealous that Leo got all this?"

Montgomery shrugged. "I don't handle stress well. Can you imagine what a nightmare dealing with this place is? All the staff, the noisy tourists hanging around, and the money you have to manage. No, I never wanted anything to do with this place. Leo had the right idea by bringing in a professional to look after everything."

I risked another sip of the martini. "Isn't Julius taking over?"

He roared a laugh. "Good grief, no. I'd do a better job than him, and that's saying something. That kid will give himself an ulcer if he doesn't learn to relax. I don't think he's given himself a day off in his life. He's always chasing after some new scheme or trying to figure out how to run things. Why bother? Give someone else the job and take the profits."

"Julius seemed convinced that he's now looking after the estate."

"I don't see it happening," Montgomery said. "And I'm going to have to step up a bit more now. Cordelia's been hinting that she's going to stop my allowance if I don't start working for it. She mentioned me becoming the entertainment manager."

"That could be... interesting."

"I can't think of anything worse." He grimaced. "But the work will fit with my hours. I'm a night owl, so you'll never see me about much before noon. And I do enjoy a good party."

"That might not be the sort of thing Lady Cordelia was thinking of. I expect she wants to see events for families and children not boozy soirees and late-night parties."

"You're probably right. What about you, Lorna Shadow. Do you like to play?" Montgomery twirled a strand of my hair around his finger.

"I do with the right person." I inched away from Montgomery. "In particular, my boyfriend."

"Ah! You've got one of those." He focused on his drink. "That's disappointing. I suppose you're blissfully happy with this chap?"

"I am. We're buying a house together."

"That's horribly serious," Montgomery said. His expression brightened and he gave me a wicked grin. "What about Helen? Is she single?"

I paused as I considered the question. She was, but Helen liked Gunner, no matter how much she denied it.

"Your hesitation is making me interested. Please tell me she's a party girl. I've been looking for someone to have some fun with. My nephew and niece are more of a nuisance than anything else. And now Leo's gone, I'm all alone. Partying on your own isn't much fun."

"It's complicated," I said. "There is someone on the scene, but they aren't together. I think it's only a matter of time before something happens."

"Which means that Helen's technically single," Montgomery said. "I should ask her out before I miss the opportunity."

"You might like to rethink that idea. The person who's interested in her is a police officer. It's not wise to tread on his toes."

Montgomery downed half of his drink and hiccupped. "Hmmm. Good point. I don't want to mess with a cop's totty. Fair enough, you're both out of bounds. If anything changes, let me know." He winked at me.

I smiled over the rim of my glass. Montgomery was an incorrigible flirt, but nothing more. "Will do. Did you and Leo often go out partying?"

"When we were younger, but there's a sixteen year age gap between us. As he got older, he wanted to play less.

Or maybe Cordelia didn't like him going out with me. Whatever the reason, he spent more and more time with his cats. Better that than hanging out with Cordelia, I suppose."

"And now Lady Cordelia is going to get rid of them," I said. "It's so sad."

Montgomery took my glass and refilled it before returning to his seat. "There's something of a mystery there."

"What kind of mystery?" I took the glass and leaned closer.

"Cordelia has been secretive in regards to Leo's will. I was sure he'd updated it. He mentioned to me something about leaving things for a friend. But he was elusive and I couldn't get much out of him. At the time, I wondered if he'd found himself a new lady, someone sweeter than Cordelia."

"Did you ever see him with another woman?"

"No, and he didn't mention her by name. But he told me he wanted to rewrite his will so the cats would be properly cared for as would his new friend. I pressed him on it, but he wouldn't give me any more information. He did say something about wanting this friend to help with the cats. That would have been a part of the deal."

"And you think Lady Cordelia is hiding this information?" I asked. "Could she have this new will and not be telling people about it?"

"I haven't got a clue," Montgomery said. "All I know is what Leo told me. I was surprised when his will was read and there was no mention of this mysterious friend."

"If you don't mind me asking, how did Leo divide his assets?"

"Just as everyone thought he would. Cordelia was to take over the estate. There were trust funds for the children, and a small amount of money for me. Although I wish it had been more. There was nothing about this friend person or the cats. That shocked me."

"How could Lady Cordelia hide this new will?" I asked. "Won't there be copies stored with a solicitor?"

"Money has power." Montgomery tapped the side of his nose. "If she wanted the will to vanish, she could make it happen. Her uncle runs the law firm that deals with all the family business."

I wasn't so sure wills could simply vanish. Since Montgomery was being so open, I decided to push my luck and ask more questions. "You don't think something bad happened to Leo?" I watched him intently. After all, I did have him on my suspect list.

He laughed. "You do have dark thoughts. Do you think someone got rid of Leo so they could get their hands on his cash?"

I looked around the expensively decorated room. "Money does make people do strange things."

"Then you'd better include me if you think something like that happened," Montgomery said. "I'm poor since Leo died. And if Cordelia carries out her threat to cut me off if I don't start working for the estate, I'll be in dire straits. Women don't chase after poor men, so I need a lot of cash to keep the ladies happy."

I chewed on my bottom lip. For all his bluster, Montgomery did care for Leo. I wasn't getting any sense that he killed his only brother. "Just assuming that someone did want to hurt Leo, who would you put at the top of your suspect list?"

"Whoever's got the most to gain from him dying." Montgomery sat up straight in his seat, his martini glass shaking slightly in his hand. "Hang on! You're being serious? Do you really think somebody hurt Leo?"

I placed my glass down and clasped my hands together. I wasn't going to reveal to Montgomery that his brother's ghost was the reason I was investigating his death. "Leo wasn't old when he died. I was surprised to learn he'd been smothered by a cat."

Montgomery scratched his hand through his messy blond hair. "It's not a typical way to die. Still, I can't imagine anyone in this family being mean enough to actually hurt Leo. I don't think he ever fell out with anybody. Well, he never had a serious argument with them. And he was never the sort to go to bed on an argument. Even when Cordelia was being a proper hag to him, he'd smooth things over."

"I'm sure it's nothing," I said. "I'm known for having an overactive imagination."

Montgomery raised his eyebrows. "That's something I'd be interested in exploring."

I shook my head, my cheeks heating up as Montgomery's grin widened. "It's not as exciting as you're picturing in your head."

He laughed and downed the rest of his drink, before slapping his thighs and standing. "Enough of this serious talk about cats, my horrible sister-in-law, and theories about who'd want to snuff out my brother. Let me see how good you are at playing pool."

I took another sip of my drink, before accepting the pool cue Montgomery handed me. As I watched him rack the balls and take the first shot, I mulled over our conversation. The missing will could be crucial in Leo's death. Lady Cordelia would have benefited from hiding the updated will to avoid missing out on some of the estate and the cats having to stay.

I needed to find a copy of this new will and reveal what it had to say.

Chapter 11

The sound of grinding gears and shouting woke me the next morning. I gave Flipper a quick cuddle before hopping out of bed and peering out the window to see what was going on.

In front of the house, stood three white vans and a yellow digger.

I dressed quickly and hurried out of my room, almost colliding with Helen as I did so.

"What's all that noise about?" she asked. "I was having a lovely dream about a prince coming to rescue me from an evil dragon. The prince was all buff and hunky and kept bossing me around in his posh voice."

I grinned. "Have you found any princes in the castle yet so you can live out that particular fantasy?"

"None that aren't mounted on the wall in a painting," Helen said. "The lack of eligible bachelors around here is an annoyance."

"You're not interested in Julius? He's posh."

"He's a child!" Helen said.

"He must be at least twenty."

"That's way too young for me," Helen said. "Anyway, what's going on outside?"

"It looks like they're having some work done on the estate," I said. "Shall we go and see what they're up to?"

Helen nodded, and we headed to the main castle door and outside. I spotted three workmen in fluorescent jackets wandering about between the vans.

"Look! It's Julius," Helen said.

Julius stood in front of one of the workmen, a clipboard in one hand and a phone against his ear. I couldn't hear what he was saying, but his tone sounded petulant and was too high-pitched to be anything good.

The man next to him kept shaking his head and frowning. Whatever was going on it didn't look like great news.

"What's he up to?" I said. "I hope it's got nothing to do with his animal park plans. This place isn't set up for the arrival of tigers."

Julius threw his clipboard to the ground and gestured wildly at the man in front of him.

"Montgomery told me that Julius needs to calm down or he'll make himself unwell," I said as I watched him jabbing his finger at the other man.

"When did you speak to Montgomery?" Helen asked.

"Yesterday evening."

"I wondered what happened to you. I had to eat dinner alone."

"The sacrifice was worth it," I said. "As was my martini headache this morning. Montgomery was very chatty and had useful information about a potential missing will."

"A missing will! Does he have any idea what this will said?"

"We had a few guesses, but he wasn't sure. There was mention of a secret friend of Leo's and some money for the cats. Montgomery thinks Lady Cordelia is hiding the will so she doesn't lose out."

"That's another good reason for Lady Cordelia to kill Leo," Helen said. "If she thought she was going to be swindled out of money by a bunch of cats, she'd want to put a stop to that."

Julius yelped, and I looked over to see a workman had him by his jacket lapels. "Come on. It looks like Julius needs saving."

"If you think I'm going to take orders from you, you jumped-up little brat, then you can think again." The muscled workman who had Julius by the collar was resting his forehead against his.

I could smell the testosterone in the air as we approached.

"It's what you're paid to do," Julius squeaked. "I'm your boss."

"No you're not," the workman said.

"Is there a problem?" I asked as I reached Julius's side. I could see his legs were shaking.

"This little shrimp needs to learn some manners," the workman said, not taking his angry glare off Julius. "He's ordering me around like he owns me."

"Bruce, be reasonable. You need to do what I tell you if this is going to work," Julius said. "All I asked was that you start on the foundation work this week."

"And I told you that's not possible," Bruce said, his dark eyes narrowing. "We have a schedule here. Those foundations don't get started for another two months."

"I've already ordered the giraffes!"

"You've done what?" Helen said.

"I got a good deal on two giraffes from a zoo who needed to get rid of them." Julius struggled in Bruce's grip, but he refused to let go.

"Maybe you need to take a break." I touched Bruce's muscled forearm as he growled at Julius.

He shot me an angry stare but then let out a sigh and dropped his hold on Julius. "This guy doesn't know what he's doing. If we start those foundations now, the security measures for the lions won't be ready in time. You'll have caged lions with no outside space. It won't be safe for anyone, and it won't be right for the big cats. I've done this sort of work before. They don't do well in enclosed spaces."

"Big cats and giraffes," Helen said. "I thought the animal park was only an idea?"

Julius brushed down his jacket and frowned at Bruce. "You can go."

Bruce took a step toward Julius and he scuttled backward.

"We'll try to calm him down for you," I muttered to Bruce. "I'm sure he's just made a mistake."

Bruce scrubbed a hand across his stubble. "I'll pull my men off this job if I have to. We don't get treated like slaves. Our work is first class." He stalked away, shooting menacing glares over his shoulder at Julius as he did so.

"I knew I'd made a mistake hiring him." Julius retrieved his clipboard and brushed dirt off it. "He's supposed to be an expert when it comes to creating new wildlife parks. The man doesn't know what he's doing."

"You're really doing it?" I asked Julius. "The animal park is happening?"

"Of course," he said. "I've been planning it for ages. I talked about it with father several times, but he never took me seriously. Now, I get the chance to prove I can create something from this failing place."

"The castle looks like it's doing alright to me," Helen said. "There's already a queue of visitors." She pointed to the long line of people waiting by the ticket office.

Julius shrugged. "Those people pay for the basics, but we have to expand and grow our income. The animal park will ensure we can do that. I have everything in hand. Although I need to get a better work crew. I'm not going to work with that idiot."

I looked over to where the workmen were gathered, muttering to each other and staring at Julius. It seemed like the feeling was mutual.

"Is Lady Cordelia happy with the animal park?" I asked. "She didn't seem so certain when we had dinner together the other night."

"Mommy's far too busy with her toy boy to care what goes on here," Julius said. "Besides, I'm in charge. Father left the estate in my hands."

I was sure that wasn't true. If what Montgomery said last night was reliable, Lady Cordelia inherited everything at Gillan Castle.

"Will your animal park include the cat sanctuary?" I asked.

"Definitely not. Those ratty old things will have to go," Julius said. "I have plans to put alpacas on that site and offer people an alpaca trek experience. People love that sort of thing."

"Won't the big cats eat the alpacas?" Helen asked.

"And the people walking the alpacas," I said.

"They'll all be separated." Julius gave an irritated sigh as he looked at his clipboard. "I do know what I'm doing."

I doubted that from what I'd heard so far. "There must be room for the cats. You've got plenty of acres here to fit everything in. People can never resist a sad-faced cat. It could be another feature of the animal park. Maybe you could have a cat café. People could take tea and cake with the unloved pussycats."

"There's no room for those cats," Julius said, not bothering to look up from his clipboard. "Every acre is accounted for. Alongside the animals, there will be visitor lodges so people can spend a weekend here. There will also be lodges for the additional staff and places to store machinery and feed for the animals. I can't have domestic cats taking up valuable space. No one will be interested in them. They're boring."

A three-legged black and white cat limped toward us. Flipper walked over to greet it. The cat was initially cautious, but they were soon bobbing heads, and it followed Flipper when he returned to my side.

"You see that thing there." Julius pointed at the cat. "Absolutely pointless. Who's going to be interested in seeing a bag of fleas like that? All that thing does is eat and poop and then expects someone to clear up after it." He kicked at the cat.

Helen shoved Julius in the shoulder. "Don't you dare try to hurt that beautiful creature! How can it defend itself against you? It's only got three legs."

"They're a nuisance." Julius glowered at Helen as he rubbed his shoulder. "And I'm glad Mommy has come to her senses and is getting rid of them. Father was obsessed with those animals, but they only irritated my allergies." He took a step toward the cat.

Flipper's hackles raised and he growled at Julius and lowered his head, his teeth bared.

"None of us like the idea of the cats leaving," I said.

"I don't care what any of you like." Julius waved a hand at me, his gaze settling on the workmen who were watching us with interest. "I've got those cretins to deal with. I can't waste any more time with you." He stalked away without a backward glance.

"I hope Bruce punches him." Helen bent and tickled under the cat's chin.

"Me too," I said. "And this time, I won't step in and stop him."

"Is my brother annoying you?"

I turned to see Tabitha walking toward us sporting a big bandage on her head and the beginnings of a black eye.

"What happened to you?" I asked.

"The stupid brakes on my car failed." Tabitha's fingers went to the bandage. "I could have died. I spun right off the road last night. I've only just got out of the hospital."

"That's terrible," Helen said. "Was anyone else hurt?"

"I was alone," Tabitha said. "That'll teach me to go out driving by myself. I never was any good behind the wheel but couldn't be bothered to wait for the cab to turn up. I'll have to rely on Mommy's chauffeur more. At least it means I can go out and have a few drinks and not worry about getting caught when I'm a bit worse for wear."

"Were you drunk when you lost control?" I asked, my initial sympathy for Tabitha waning.

She sniffed. "Absolutely not. I was on my way to a drink's party if you must know. I'd barely had a drop before I left. Gin threes at the most."

"You were lucky not to be badly injured," I said. "Or to hurt anyone else."

Tabitha shrugged. "Tell me about it. I stamped on the brake pedal several times, but it didn't respond. I hit a sharp bend and ran right off the road. I woke up a few minutes later with a bump on my head and double vision."

"I'm glad it was nothing more serious," Helen said. "These country roads can be tricky to navigate."

"True enough. Not that anyone around here cares what happens to me," Tabitha said. "If Daddy was still here, he'd have taken the best care of me. All Mommy said when she found out what had happened was to get a cab home when I was ready to leave the hospital. She didn't even come to see if I was all right. As for Julius, he's got his head buried so far into this animal park idea that he wouldn't care if I was dead or alive."

"I'm sure that's not true," I said.

"It is. Not that I care about him. Julius is a joke around here. He reckons he's in charge of this estate, but it would fall apart if he really took over. Poor Mommy is left to do it all."

"What do you think about Julius's idea for the animal park?" I asked.

"He keeps trying to sell me on the idea, but I like the cats," she said. "I want to keep them around. I love nothing more than stroking their soft fur and cuddling them. And I know Daddy would like that. We always enjoyed spending time with the cats, just me and him. It was our favorite thing to do together."

Big Ginge rushed out from behind a bush and ran toward Flipper and the three-legged cat.

Tabitha clicked her fingers at Big Ginge and beckoned him to her. "Here pretty kitty."

Big Ginge's hackles raised. He hissed at Tabitha and swiped a paw at her.

"That one has always hated me." Tabitha sighed dramatically. "The other cats are all fine. That one was always Daddy's favorite and wouldn't have anything to do with anyone else."

I exchanged a glance with Helen. Big Ginge had been friendly to us the moment we'd discovered him in my bedroom. And he kept appearing when we were around and asking for a head rub. I couldn't figure out why he wasn't friendly with Tabitha. Unless she'd done something to make him wary of her. Mistreat a cat once and they'll always remember.

"Are you going to fight to keep the cats here?" I asked Tabitha. "It would be a nice legacy for your dad if you did."

She shrugged and inspected her fingernails. "I'm not sure I can be bothered. They're nice to have around, but Mommy's convinced they need to go. I hate fighting with her. Maybe Julius is right, an animal park will bring in more money. And I've got some big plans for next year. I'm getting married."

"Who are you engaged to?" Helen asked.

"I'm not serious with any one person right now," Tabitha said. "I always knew I'd get married when I was twenty-five. That's next year. Therefore, Mommy needs to put aside a heap of money for my wedding. And I'll need a house of my own in the countryside. The apartment in London won't be suitable for a married woman."

I stifled a smile. "You've got your whole life planned out."

"Of course I have. I can't spend my life drifting around this crumbling old place. Julius is welcome to it, whatever he decides to do. He can paint it pink and turn it into a fairy castle. Actually, that's not a bad idea." She tried to stroke the three-legged cat, but it swiftly limped out of her way.

"A fairy castle!" Helen shook her head.

"Whatever. I don't care." Tabitha's brow wrinkled as she glared at the cat. "I don't know what's wrong with these animals today. Well, I'm out for lunch so I need to go get ready." She gave us a finger wave and strode back to the house.

"For someone who claims to like cats so much, they don't think much of her," Helen said.

"That's just what I was thinking," I said. "Maybe she's not as nice to them as she reckons she is when no one else is around. Or maybe a cat saw Tabitha doing something she shouldn't."

"You think the cats have warned each other to stay away from Tabitha?" Helen grinned. "I know cats are clever, but I'm not sure they're up to that."

"Don't be daft. But she could be feeling guilty and is giving off a strange vibe the cats are picking up on. They're sensitive to human emotions just like dogs."

"A guilty vibe as in I-killed-my father-and-am-trying-to-conceal-the-fact sort of thing?"

"Why not? If there was a cat in the room when Tabitha smothered Leo, every time she saw a cat it would be an unpleasant reminder of what she did."

"She does give out mixed signals," Helen said. "And claiming she likes cats but then they all run away from her is weird. And she said she loves the cats but can't be bothered to fight to keep the sanctuary. That doesn't fit."

"I saw Leo in the garden yesterday. He doesn't think Tabitha has anything to do with his death, but maybe the cats know better."

"You think we should start questioning the cats?"

That comment earned Helen a shove. "No! I do think they're picking up on something strange about Tabitha, though. We need to keep an eye on her."

"A cat hating killer." Helen shivered. "I can't think of anything worse."

I shook my head. Sadly, I could, and we'd met a few of them in the past. "Come on, we need to get to work, or Lady Cordelia will start complaining."

We'd have to figure out exactly how Tabitha was involved with her dad's death later.

Chapter 12

I'd been on the phone for three hours, contacting all the animal sanctuaries I'd located in an attempt to find homes for our unwanted cats. Things weren't going well.

"And you're sure you've got no spare cages? You can't even take half a dozen cats from us?"

"I'm sorry my love," the elderly lady on the other end of the phone said. "I wish I could help you, but there are so many animals needing our assistance. It sounds like you've got a good setup already. I'm sure you can keep them for a bit longer."

"I really need your help. The owner of the sanctuary is considering having the cats put to sleep if I can't find them somewhere else to go."

"That's a shame," the woman said. "I wish I could magic up more room. I've got your details and will give you a call if we get any vacancies. But we have a waiting list of three months. We're not going to be able to assist you."

I briefly considered begging, I was so desperate to find places for the cats, but knew the lady was doing her best. We said our goodbyes and I slumped in my seat.

Every conversation had been the same. There were so many unloved animals and no room for them.

Lady Cordelia walked into the study and raised her eyebrows when she saw me. "Don't you have any work to do?"

I tapped the list in front of me and sat up straight. "I've been working my way through these animal sanctuaries. So far, none of them can help us with the cats. It looks like they're here to stay for a while."

"What have you offered them?" Lady Cordelia asked.

"Well, I've offered them the cats," I said. "What else was I supposed to offer?"

"Give me that list." Lady Cordelia snatched up the list of sanctuaries before I could pass it to her. "You do realize these are all charities?"

"I do," I said.

"And charities are always in need of money."

I slowly exhaled. I must not lose my temper with my employer. "You want me to bribe them into taking the cats?"

"Not a bribe. Simply offer a generous donation and a few cats at the same time." Lady Cordelia smiled thinly. "By helping us with our cat problem, we can help them."

"I don't want the charities put under pressure to take the cats," I said. "They're all full."

"They'll be fine. Let me show you how it's done." Lady Cordelia picked up the phone and dialed a telephone number on the list, before shooting me a cold smile. "Everybody has a price. We just need to find out what the charities price is and offer it to them."

I nodded and looked at Flipper who was snoozing in a patch of afternoon sunshine that filtered in through the window. I had to remember this was for the cats. If a bribe was what it took to get them new homes then I'd just have to ignore the uncomfortable feeling in my stomach and let it happen.

"Hello. This is Lady Cordelia Babington. I would like to offer a donation to your charity." She nodded and tapped her neat coral painted nails on the desk.

"Yes, I know how good the cause is and what excellent work you do. And I'd like to offer you a donation of five thousand pounds."

From where I was sitting, I could hear the excited babble of the person on the other end of the phone. I guessed they didn't get that kind of offer too often.

"That's all very good," Lady Cordelia said. "And I wonder if you might do me a tiny favor in return for this donation. I have six cats who need new homes. They have all been well looked after but there is no longer a suitable place for them to live. If you can help me out with that, I'd appreciate it. I can send them along with the donation."

I really hoped the person on the other end of the phone would realize what Lady Cordelia was doing. The smile on her face suggested otherwise.

"That's excellent," Lady Cordelia said, her smile turning smug. "I'll have the money and the cats with you soon." She placed the phone down and looked at me. "You see. Offer them something they need and they'll do anything for you."

I nodded. It still didn't feel right, bribing desperate charities who needed money, and then adding conditions to that donation.

"Can I trust you to get back to the other sanctuaries you've contacted and see if a little money will make the cats disappear that bit quicker?" Lady Cordelia handed me back the list.

"I'll make a start on the calls," I said.

She walked around to the other side of her desk and pulled out a chair. "Oh, for goodness sake!"

I looked up in surprise at her outburst. "What is it?"

"One of those wretched cats has been in here and left an enormous hairball on my seat." Her nose wrinkled as she backed away from the chair.

I fought hard not to smile. It was as if the cats knew Lady Cordelia no longer wanted them and were having a little own revenge on her. Good for them if that was the case. I hoped there'd be plenty more hairballs appearing on Lady Cordelia's seat, along with a few well targeted piles of vomit in some of her designer shoes.

There was a knock on the study door. Sebastien poked his head in. "I hope I'm not disturbing you." He smiled when he saw me.

"Sebastien, darling. It's lovely to see you." Lady Cordelia hurried over to him, smoothing down her sleek hair as she did so.

"I wanted to see if you were free to go for a late lunch or an early dinner," Sebastien said. "What would you call an early dinner? Afternoon tea?"

Lady Cordelia played with Sebastien's hair as he spoke. I watched with interest as he struggled not to flinch. She needed to stop fussing over him like he was a toy or their relationship wouldn't last.

"That's a perfect idea." Lady Cordelia looked over at me. "Can I rely on you to get on with the work I've given you? Don't take no for an answer from any of those charities."

"What are you doing?" Sebastien asked.

"Getting the cats rehomed," I said.

He frowned. "Why? I like having the cats around."

I was surprised to hear that. Sandy had suggested he was the reason Lady Cordelia wanted them gone.

"We can keep one or two if you really have to have a cat around," Lady Cordelia said. "We've got too many, though. And they remind me of Leo. It's time I moved on."

He nodded. "I understand that. I imagine you'll do what's best for the animals and make sure they all get wonderful places to live."

I pinched my lips together. She wouldn't if she had her own way.

"Of course. Now, let's talk about something interesting," Lady Cordelia said as she guided Sebastien to the door. "We need a romantic weekend away together."

"Just the two of us?" Sebastien tugged at the collar of his shirt.

"It wouldn't be all that romantic if I brought along the staff as well." She flashed me a smile. "Paris is lovely this time of year. Or we could try Italy. Have you ever been? It's so beautiful."

Sebastien rubbed his forehead. "I like the idea of getting away from it all, but I've got a lot on right now."

"We could make it a romantic winter getaway instead." Lady Cordelia wrapped an arm around Sebastien's waist, seeming to forget I was in the room. "Just imagine the two of us in front of a roaring fire, sipping mulled wine and enjoying ourselves. We so rarely get to spend any time together."

I focused on the list of animal sanctuaries and tried to tune out their conversation, just in case Lady Cordelia started sweet talking in poor Sebastien's ear.

"I'll check my diary and see when I'm available," he said. "But you know I have commitments."

"If it's only your silly charity duties. You shouldn't worry about that," Lady Cordelia said. "You don't have to volunteer for them. It's not as if they pay you."

"I do it because I want to," Sebastien said, his tone sharp. "I get a lot out of doing my charity work. I can't let them down just because you want to go away and have fun."

"No. Well, think about it," Lady Cordelia said. "We've been together a while now, and we've yet to have a vacation. It will be my treat. You don't have to worry about a thing."

"I'll definitely think about it." Sebastien's phone rang. He pulled it out of his jacket pocket and looked at the caller display. "I need to take this."

Lady Cordelia watched Sebastien leave the room, a girly smile on her face.

As much as she was into Sebastien, I got the impression he was lukewarm in returning her affections. I could understand him getting annoyed by her clinging and constant fussing, but he almost seemed repulsed by her.

Maybe Julius and Tabitha were onto something when they claimed that Sebastien was only in this relationship for the money and free vacations.

"I need to make some private phone calls before I go out with Sebastien." Lady Cordelia pulled out her chair and grimaced as she saw the hairball again. "Give me twenty minutes, then you can get on with your own duties."

"Of course." I hopped up from my seat and headed to the door.

Flipper was still soundly sleeping in the sun, so I left him to it and hurried out in search of Sebastien.

I wanted to talk to him and see if I could figure out what he was really doing with Lady Cordelia. If he wasn't in this relationship for love, and had decided to target Lady Cordelia for her money, he'd have needed to get rid of Leo before standing a chance of getting access to the estate and all its wealth.

I had a quick look in the downstairs rooms, but he wasn't in any of them. I pulled open the front door and walked into the autumnal afternoon.

I could hear a man talking, and as I hurried closer, I realized it was Sebastien.

He appeared around the corner of the building, then turned and paced away.

I ducked behind a bush before he saw me and listened to his conversation.

"I can't do this any longer," he said. "She's getting too much."

I raised my eyebrows. He must mean Lady Cordelia.

"She's talking about us going away together, just the two of us. Can you imagine what it would be like trapped in a room with that woman? I don't think I'd come out alive."

Wow! He really didn't like her.

"And you know what she's going to make me do." Sebastien's tone was mournful. "I've made as many excuses as possible, including the one where I want to save myself until after we're married. That only made her start hassling me into giving her a ring. I thought she'd get bored of me after a couple of months and I'd be able to get us what we need and escape before things got too serious. She's acting like some starry-eyed teenager."

Although Lady Cordelia could be a bit of a bitch, I felt a sliver of sympathy for her. From the sounds of it, Sebastien really was using her.

"I'd better go. I promised I'd take her out this afternoon. Maybe I can get her so drunk she passes out and I can have the night off. Honestly, she's got arms like an octopus. I'm always finding her hand on my backside or somewhere else it shouldn't be."

I shoved my hand over my mouth. I wasn't sure who I felt sorrier for, Sebastien or Lady Cordelia.

"That's not funny!" he said. "You try being in a relationship with Lady Cordelia and see how much work it is."

I jumped as something soft and silky pushed past my legs. It was a skinny gray cat with enormous amber eyes. It gave a soft meow and blinked up at me.

I pressed my finger to my lips, hoping the cat wouldn't give away my position and reveal me to Sebastian.

The cat meowed louder and pawed at my leg.

I knelt and stroked the cat, hoping to keep her quiet, but it only made her more excited. I shooed the cat gently away, but she refused to budge, and danced out from behind the bush. She looked back at me and made a loud high-pitched meow.

I winced and ducked.

"Lorna! What are you doing behind the shrubbery?"

Chapter 13

I scrambled out from behind the bush, trying to make my sudden appearance look completely normal and not as if I'd been eavesdropping on Sebastien's private conversation. "Oh! I was just admiring the... foliage."

"I didn't know anybody was out here." He looked at the phone in his hand. "I was talking to a close friend."

I decided to come clean. "Sorry, but I sort of heard some of your conversation. It sounded like more than a friend to me. It also sounded like you don't think much of Lady Cordelia, even though you're supposed to be dating."

"No! You misunderstood what you heard," he sputtered.

"Then explain it to me. Why are you seeing Lady Cordelia if you don't like her?"

"Oh dear. I mean, I am fond of Cordelia." Sebastien scuffed his polished shoe across the gravel. "It's just that she can be... difficult at times."

"You're taking advantage of her," I said. "Lady Cordelia doesn't deserve that. If you're only using her, you should end things before she gets hurt. She likes you. You shouldn't lead her on."

He ran a hand through his hair. "This has gotten out of control. I never wanted to cause anybody pain. I'm hurting myself, Cordelia, and Elton."

"Who's Elton?"

"My... well that is to say, my, erm... boyfriend." Sebastien dropped his gaze to the ground. "He's wonderful. He's an artist but is struggling for money."

"You and Elton decided to take advantage of Lady Cordelia and get your hands on her cash?" I asked. "That's a terrible thing to do. She must be lonely after Leo died. You've manipulated that."

"I know that's true. And I don't feel good about it," he said, not looking at me. "It was Elton's idea. Last year, he was commissioned to do a couple of pieces for Leo, portraits of some of the cats from the sanctuary who'd died. He wanted a memorial for them. When Elton was here, he saw how wealthy the family was. He needs start-up capital so he can establish himself as an artist, get a new studio, and a whole host of materials."

"He should go out and earn money to pay for all of that, not extort it from a lonely widow."

"I've suggested that, and I help him when I can, but you heard Cordelia say I don't make much money. I volunteer at a number of charities because I love the work they do. I'm dependent on Cordelia, and Elton's dependent on me to get enough money to keep us both going."

"What were you planning to do?" I asked. "Steal from Lady Cordelia?"

Sebastien waved his hands at me. "Not so loud! Someone might hear."

"And you wouldn't want that!"

"No, I wouldn't." He sighed. "I wasn't going to steal. I was going to ask for investment in a business idea. We haven't gotten all the details figured out, but we were creating a business plan to make everything legitimate. If we could get our hands on half a million, we could head off somewhere exotic like Hawaii or even Thailand, buy a place, and Elton could do his art while I focused on my volunteering. We'd both be happy."

"Lady Cordelia would be miserable, though," I said. "And she'd be down half a million. That sounds a lot like stealing to me."

"Cordelia has many millions in the bank," Sebastien said. "I've seen some of the bank statements. I know she wouldn't miss the money."

"She would miss you. She is fond of you. It would break her heart if you decided to leave."

"I realize that now," he said. "When we first started this, I saw things the same as Elton. Cordelia was just an entitled, privileged rich woman who spent her money on ridiculously expensive pieces of furniture and designer clothes. She should be investing it into helping others, or giving money to charity. I sometimes have to prise the money out of her fingers for the causes we're involved in. She doesn't give anything away without getting something back that benefits her."

I nodded as I recalled how Lady Cordelia used her donation to the animal sanctuary to get what she needed.

"You aren't going to tell her about me, are you?" Sebastien's face was pinched with worry.

I sighed before shaking my head. "No. You should tell her what you're doing, though."

He grabbed hold of my hand. "I know it's wrong, and I will make amends. I'll let her down gently. Let her know we can't keep seeing each other. Perhaps I could say I've been offered a volunteering opportunity in deepest darkest Africa. I know she'll never follow me out there. She likes to stick to her European breaks."

"Let her down gently, and do it without stealing from her," I said.

"Elton will be so unhappy with me if I don't get any money, though." Sebastien's bottom lip jutted out. "He was relying on this to change our lives."

"Then get the money honestly," I said. "Elton can get a job. So can you, and start saving. That's what everyone else does."

"I know, you're right," he said. "But Elton's so sensitive. I don't think he'd be able to handle a real job."

"He should try," I said. "They're not that bad. Well, providing you don't get the boss from hell. Stealing isn't going to solve your problems. You'll only end up behind bars."

"I'm worried that if I tell Cordelia what's going on, she might get revenge on me," Sebastien said. "She has got a temper on her, especially when she doesn't get her own way."

"She'll be angry and upset with you, but I can't imagine she'll do anything bad."

Sebastien glanced up at the house. "I'm not so sure. What about Leo?"

My eyebrows shots up. "What's Leo got to do with this?"

"I don't think his death was accidental." He chewed on a manicured nail. "What if Cordelia had something to do with it?"

I took a step closer. "What do you know that makes you think that?"

Sebastien looked around. "Nothing for sure, but Cordelia told me that she needed to stop Leo changing his will. He'd decided to leave money to different people and set up a charity so the cats in the sanctuary would be cared for after he died."

"And Lady Cordelia was unhappy about that?"

"She tolerates the cats, but I don't think she likes them," he said. "And with the changes to the will, she'd have been down a lot of money and would have had to keep the animals. Leo was planning to set up the sanctuary so it would run in perpetuity. Cordelia would never have been able to shut it down."

That was a perfect motive for murder. "Has Lady Cordelia ever told you she did something to Leo?"

"No! But she talks about being glad he's gone. She also told me their marriage wasn't a happy one. She even thought he might be seeing somebody else."

I'd heard that rumor before, and it was something I needed to look into. A mistress should be on the suspect list if one existed. "I think you could be right about Leo's death not being an accident."

Sebastien swallowed loudly. "If I break things off with her, she could come after me and Elton."

I arched a brow. "Maybe you deserve it. You were planning to steal from her."

"I've been such an idiot," he said. "What should I do?"

"How about you help me figure out what really happened to Leo? If you do, I'll keep your secret."

"You won't tell Cordelia anything?" Sebastien's face lit up.

"I won't tell her, but you need to deal with it. You can't keep stringing her along, it's not fair."

"Even if she had something to do with Leo's death?"

"If she killed Leo, that's something the police will deal with. It doesn't mean that you can get away with taking money from her and manipulating her affections."

He sighed and looked at the ground. "I hope Elton still wants me after I do this."

"Sebastien, you're a lovely guy. If Elton really does want to be with you, he'll stay whether you're wealthy or poor. And if he does decide to leave, at least you'll know he was only in it for the money."

"I can't bear that thought." His hand went to his stomach and his face paled. "He could be using me just like I've been using Cordelia. I feel terrible."

"And that's exactly how Lady Cordelia will feel if she discovers what you're doing," I said. "So, will you help me figure out what happened to Leo and let Lady Cordelia down as gently as possible? Do we have a deal?"

"We do," Sebastien said. "Where do you want to start?"

Chapter 14

I felt emboldened now I had someone else on my side to assist with the search for Leo's killer. "We need to find an up-to-date copy of Leo's will."

"The will. Good thinking." Sebastien rubbed his chin.

"Any ideas where that might be?" I asked.

"It could be in Cordelia's bedroom." He shuddered and glanced at an upstairs window. "I try to avoid going in there whenever I can. She's very frisky for an older woman."

"Can you sneak me in there now? Lady Cordelia's on the phone, which means we've got a few minutes to look around before she expects me back in her office."

Sebastien nodded, and we hurried back into the house. "Let's go now before I change my mind. She keeps some private papers in her bedroom, but I've never paid them much attention."

After a quick check to make sure the way was clear, we dashed up the stairs. Sebastien hurried me along the corridor and into a sage-green and cream bedroom with an enormous four-poster bed and expensive antique furniture.

"I'll keep a lookout by the door and alert you if anyone's coming," Sebastien said.

I hurried to a cabinet in the corner of the room and rifled swiftly through the drawers.

"You didn't seem surprised when I revealed my worries about Leo's death," Sebastien said.

"I wasn't," I said.

"Why do you think something bad happened to him?"

"You might say I had a tip-off," I said.

He gasped. "Somebody else thinks Leo was killed?"

"They definitely do." I decided not to mention it was Leo himself who believed he'd been murdered.

"How awful if it was Cordelia," Sebastien said. "I've been dating a murderer."

"You've also been trying to con a murderer. You should be more worried about that."

"Good point," he said. "Have you found anything useful?"

I closed the drawers on the cabinet. "Nothing so far. She might have destroyed the will to make sure there was no evidence."

"Leo was good with his money," Sebastien said. "I bet he made copies of everything important, the will included."

"Did the two of you ever meet?" I asked.

"Yes, a couple of times at charity events. He seemed like a decent guy. Absolutely besotted with his cats. We had a conversation for over an hour about them at one event. Leo was no fool. He knew his stuff and was good with investments. He even gave me a few tips for investing in different businesses."

"Then you owe it to Leo to uncover if anything bad happened to him."

Sebastien was quiet for a moment as I continued to search the room. "You do realize I have a lot to gain by Leo no longer being alive."

I turned slowly and stared at him. "That's very true. Is there something you'd like to confess to?"

"Maybe I'm the killer."

My heart pounded as I stared at his stern expression. Had I just made a huge mistake and revealed what I knew to Leo's actual killer?

Sebastien grinned at me. "You've gone really pale. The Goth look suits you."

I let out the breath I'd been holding. "Not funny. But you're right, with Leo out the way, you could start working your magic on Lady Cordelia. It gives you a good motive for murder."

"Sweetie, I'd never do such a thing," Sebastien said. "I can't even squash flies. I'm all for everyone having a shot at life. Did Cordelia tell you I'm a vegan?"

"She didn't," I said.

"She hates it, and is always serving me gross piles of dead animals. She thinks real men eat meat. I read a study that claims eating meat actually lowers testosterone levels. And I need as much of that as I can get. I'm hoping to have a child with Elton one day. Well, a surrogate will carry the baby, but I'll be the father."

"That sounds wonderful," I said.

"So, I don't hurt any animals, and I definitely don't hurt people. Even ones with arms like an octopus." He grimaced.

I was convinced enough by his argument that I turned my back and had a look through the final drawer in the bedroom. I let out a frustrated sigh. "There's nothing here. Does Lady Cordelia have any private rooms she uses?"

Sebastien squeaked and dashed from the door, flapping his arms at me. "You need to hide. Cordelia's coming!"

I looked around the room for a suitable place to conceal myself, before racing to the closet. I pulled open the door and jumped inside, hiding behind a row of dresses just in time. A second later, I heard the bedroom door open.

"Darling! What a lovely surprise," Lady Cordelia said. "What are you doing in here? Hoping for a little afternoon delight, you naughty boy?"

I clamped my hand over my mouth, feeling a shred of sympathy for Sebastien at the saucy tone Lady Cordelia was using. What he was doing was wrong, but people do crazy things when they're in love, and he sounded like he'd fallen hard for Elton.

"Oh, no. Nothing like that. I was just... looking for a missing cufflink," Sebastien said.

"And there was me thinking you were planning some romantic surprise," Lady Cordelia said. "We have been together for nearly six months. I'm ready when you are."

"There's no need to rush things. We aren't even engaged," Sebastien said. "And I wouldn't want to think I'm pushing you into anything so soon after losing Leo."

"I lost Leo to those wretched animals years ago," Lady Cordelia said. "And they're the cause of all my stress at the moment. Not only that, but I'm beginning to have doubts about that new girl, Lorna."

My eyes widened and I pressed my ear to the door of the closet. What problem did she have with me?

Sebastien cleared his throat. "Why don't we go downstairs? I'll make you a cup of tea and you can tell me all about it."

"I'd much rather have a gin and tonic and go out like you suggested," Lady Cordelia said. "The problem is, Lorna doesn't seem all that good at her job. I've given her the simple task of sorting out the cat problem. So far, all she's done is create problems. Anyone would think she doesn't want the animals taken away from the estate. She's only been here five minutes, she knows nothing about what we do here. I can't understand why she's being so difficult."

"Let's get you out of here." Sebastien sounded anxious. "I fancy some fresh air."

"She wasn't even prepared to attempt some gentle bribery when trying to get rid of the animals," Lady Cordelia continued. "Lorna claims to have plenty of experience dealing with the upper class, but I'm not sure she's used to being around our sort of money. Old money behaves differently to newly found wealth. I'll have to investigate her background some more and make sure she wasn't making false allegations about her experience."

My mouth fell open and my hands balled into fists. I was great at what I did.

"I'm sure she wouldn't do that," Sebastien said. "From what I know of Lorna, she seems like an honest person."

"You don't know her at all," Lady Cordelia said. "She might be playing us all for fools. She's supposed to have worked for several lords and ladies across the country. I'm going to get in touch with them and see what I can find out about Miss Shadow. She'd better pull her socks up in regards to her work ethics, or this relationship is going to come to a speedy end."

I resisted the urge to jump out of the closet and tell Lady Cordelia exactly where she could stick her job. I'd been in better paid and much more pleasant places to work than this. Just because I wasn't willing to bend the rules and bribe desperate charities to take the cats off her hands, that didn't mean I was a bad employee. I was standing up for the vulnerable. It was the right thing to do.

"Cordelia, you look stressed out," Sebastien said. "How about that fresh air?"

"No, I might take a nap," Lady Cordelia said. "I can't find Lorna. I wanted to try her on some different administration tasks to see if she's good at anything she claims to be. If she keeps hiding like this, then she's going to have to go."

I pressed my lips together. I was hiding right at that moment, but I didn't have much choice. If Lady Cordelia caught me snooping into the very real possibility that she'd killed her husband, I'd be out of this job before I'd gotten started.

"I need a hug," Lady Cordelia said.

My toes curled at the girly tone she used on Sebastien. No wonder he cringed every time she got near him.

"Better not. I think I'm coming down with a cold," Sebastien said. "Don't get too close, in case I'm infectious."

"Darling, you always seem to have colds these days," Lady Cordelia said. "I'm going to ask my doctor to give you a thorough medical and make sure you don't have anything more serious. Are you sure you get enough protein in your diet? All those chickpeas and lentil burgers can't be good for you."

"I get all the protein I need," Sebastien said.

"Well, I don't mind your cold germs," Lady Cordelia said. "Come and give me a squish."

I cringed as I heard slurpy kissing noises. If this went on for much longer, I'd have to reveal myself. I couldn't stay here if things got hot and heavy between them.

Lady Cordelia let out a sigh. "I feel better already."

"Let's go and find you that gin," Sebastien said.

"It's going to need to be a strong one," Lady Cordelia said. "I just had Julius bending my ear about his animal park again. Did you see all the workmen he brought on site? I didn't say he could do that, but he's already drawn up plans and put out a contract to tender. Anyone would think he's in charge around here. He's got a lot to learn before I hand over the estate to him."

"Just make sure he doesn't get ahead of himself," Sebastien said. "You don't want him spending all your money."

"I'm not worried about that," Lady Cordelia said. "He has his own trust fund. I'm happy to give him some money for a sensible business idea. This isn't it. And Leo wouldn't approve of the park going ahead. They argued about it on several occasions. He was adamant the park shouldn't happen. He didn't want wild animals dragged in here for people's entertainment. He thought that was cruel."

The more I got to know about Leo, the more I liked him. He had a good heart when it came to animals.

I grimaced as the sound of more smooching drifted toward me. Then a loud, false-sounding sneeze came from Sebastien.

"Darling! You must be coming down with something after all," Lady Cordelia said.

"I did warn you I had the sniffles," Sebastien said. "We'd better lay off the kissing for a bit. I don't want you to get sick."

"You could be right," Lady Cordelia said, her tone cautious. "Let's go and find that drink, and you can have a hot toddy. That'll make you feel better."

I waited a few moments after the bedroom door had closed before jumping out of the closet. I had another quick look around the room to see if I'd missed any hiding places for the will, but turned up nothing of use.

I slipped out of the bedroom and back down the stairs. I hadn't found the will, but what Lady Cordelia had said about Julius and his insistence on the animal park, raised my interest in him again as a suspect.

If Leo had refused Julius any chance of having the park, he might have decided to remove the biggest obstacle in his way so he could get on with his plans.

I needed to speak to Julius again and see just how far he'd go to make his dream of the animal park a reality.

Chapter 15

I'd borrowed Helen's car for the evening, and was parked outside a large, gray-stone detached house. I was just in time to see Zach and Jessie arrive in his mud spattered Land Rover.

I gave him a wave as I hopped out the car with Flipper and joined him by the front door, kissing Zach's cheek as I did so.

Flipper and Jessie snuffled noses and then sat down.

"What do you think of the place from the outside?" Zach looped an arm around my waist. "It could do with a whitewash, but it'll look great when it's smartened up."

I looked at the wide bay windows at the front. The frames were partially rotten. "It will need a bit of money spent on it."

"But it's a bargain," Zach said. "And I don't mind putting some time in on the house if you like it. Gunner's also not bad at getting his hands dirty when I force him into action. Although he'll tell you otherwise."

"It's definitely got potential," I said.

A sleek black car pulled up and a man of about twenty-five with slick-backed blond hair and an off-the-peg suit stepped out.

"Good evening, Mr. Booth and Miss Shadow. It's nice to see you both," he said. "I'm Johnny. I'll show you around this amazing place. There's lots of room to grow, and plenty of opportunity to put your stamp on it with a bit of time and elbow grease."

We both shook hands with Johnny and waited as he jimmied the key in the lock several times, before forcing his shoulder against the door and giving it a shove. He stumbled through and skidded on a pile of uncollected mail.

"We'll need a new door," Zach muttered as he let the dogs go in ahead of us, Flipper leading the way and Jessie close behind.

"Most of the restoration work is cosmetic." Johnny straightened his tie and grinned at us. "And the hallway has a lovely wide vista. And these flagstones will scrub up to perfection."

I grinned as I inspected the grimy cracked floor. I was used to hearing the usual nonsense estate agents spoke as they tried to sell something that had been neglected.

"No problems with subsidence?" Zach asked.

"Not a problem," Johnny said. "These old buildings are usually sound." He tapped on the wall and some dust drifted off. "Nothing a good clean and some paint won't cure."

We wandered into the front living room, which was bare of any furniture, not even a carpet on the wooden floorboards.

"These will look nice varnished," I said. "Or we could put a whitewash on them."

"Good idea," Johnny said. "And you could open up the fireplace as well if you like that sort of thing. Make it a real feature of the room."

"We do like open fires," Zach said. "How long has the place been on the market?"

"About two months," Johnny said. "So, if you're thinking of making an offer, I'd suggest you do. The owner is keen on moving on. It's been in his family for years, but his mother couldn't afford to keep the repairs up."

"She didn't die here, did she?" I peered into a dark looking corner.

Johnny gave me a worried look and shook his head. "No, she became ill and was taken into a care home. The place was empty for about seven months before the son put it up for sale."

"That's good to know." I looked around the room, tuning into any ghostly vibes that might be present. I didn't sense anything.

Flipper was also relaxed as he snuffled around the floor, Jessie never far from his side.

"Come and take a look at the dining room. Then I'll show you the kitchen," Johnny said.

We followed him into another empty room and then into a dated kitchen that would need to be ripped out and replaced.

"How many bedrooms?" I asked.

"Five bedrooms," Johnny said. "Three good-sized doubles, with the potential for putting attached bathrooms in if you wanted. Then some smaller rooms, more suitable for guests, a study, or even a nursery." He flashed us a cheeky grin.

"Maybe one day," Zach murmured.

We checked out an equally dated bathroom and then headed out into an overgrown garden. It was already getting dark, but I could see there were several months of work that needed doing. But there was plenty of space for Flipper and Jessie to run around in, as they were ably demonstrating. And, with some imagination, it would be lovely.

A large shed dominated one corner of the garden, its felt roof sagging and the door hanging off its hinges. I wandered over to take a look.

As I peered through the grimy window, the face of a wizened elderly man stared back. A cold shudder slid through my veins as he jabbed his finger at me and frowned.

I looked over my shoulder to see Zach talking to Johnny about the boundary fence, before I turned back to the ghost. "I'm guessing this is your shed?" I whispered.

The ghost's eyes widened and he jabbed another finger at me.

"I'm just looking around. I hope you don't mind. We're thinking of buying your house."

The ghost shook his head and blinked out of sight.

This didn't look promising. If there was an angry ghost hiding in the garden, he might decide to appear through the walls in the house and try to scare us away.

The elderly ghost appeared in front of me. He was shorter than I was, with an old cloth cap in his hands and a scowl on his wrinkled face.

I walked farther down the garden, making sure I was out of earshot of Johnny and Zach. "We're not doing any harm. We want to find a place to live, and thought this looked nice."

The ghost frowned and then looked over at Zach and Johnny.

"They're not doing any harm by being here either," I said. "Wouldn't you like a family to move in and make the house warm and friendly again? It looks like it hasn't been loved for a long time."

The ghost's eyes narrowed before he swooped away and spun in a circle around Zach and Johnny.

I hurried over, trying to keep my panic under wraps. This ghost was getting agitated. That was never a good thing.

Zach raised his eyebrows as I got near and rubbed his hands down his arms. "It's getting cold out here."

"It sure is. It won't be long before winter arrives." Johnny gave an affable nod. "So, what do you think of the place? You can have another look round on your own if you need some more time."

Zach looked at me and nodded. "I like it. What do you think?"

"Come and check out the shed." I grabbed Zach's hand and pulled him away from Johnny.

"This shed will need taking down," Zach said as we approached it. "I can put something new up easily enough. Don't let the shed put you off."

"The shed's fine. It's what's lurking inside it that isn't so great," I said. "That cold you felt was a ghost. He's not happy with us being here."

Zach let out a sigh and ran his hands through his dark hair as he peered through the dirty window. "So, this one's not for us either?"

"I don't think so. It's a nice house but there too many negatives. I'm all for doing a bit of renovation, but we'd be doing nothing else but that for the next couple of years. It's too much work with us both having full-time jobs. And if we have to throw a pesky ghost into the mix as well, I don't think it'll be fun for anybody."

Zach looked at the house and shrugged. "Speaking of ghosts, how's it going in the castle? Any more spooks turned up to trouble you?"

"I'm still trying to figure out what's going on with my murder victim," I said. "Leo's got a lot of people who are benefiting now he's dead. It's taking time to work out who's involved."

"Just take care around the living *and* the dead," Zach said. "And keep out of trouble."

"I don't even know the meaning of the word."

He kissed my forehead and grumbled under his breath. "And as for the troublesome living, Gunner's been asking questions about Helen."

"He has?" I grinned at Zach. "Do you think they're going to get together?"

"They're both single, so it's possible. I can't decide if it's a good thing or not," he said. "Gunner's been on his own for years. He has girlfriends, but the second any of them get serious he runs in the opposite direction. And I get the impression Helen is looking for a husband."

"She is. And a posh husband at that," I said.

Zach shrugged. "Maybe they could just have some fun together."

"And that won't get awkward if we're all living under the same roof and Gunner decides he wants the fun to stop."

He shook his head. "Let's hope they can both be adults about this."

I wrinkled my nose, knowing how quickly Helen dreamed up fantasies with men after she'd only been on a couple of dates with them. "Maybe nothing will happen between them."

"Well, we don't need to referee their relationship," Zach said. "You keep me busy enough. And when there's a ghost around, I barely get a look in."

"I'm not that bad!"

Zach grinned at me. "No! You're perfect."

I turned to walk back to the house and stumbled straight through the ghost of the angry old man. Chills ran up and down my spine and a cold sweat broke out on my forehead. Flipper raced over. He jumped up at me and licked my hand, his gaze intent on mine.

"So, do you want to make an offer?" Johnny rubbed his hands together. "There are other people interested. I'd advise you to get in quickly."

I shook my head, my tongue feeling numb and my brain frozen. "This isn't the house for us. Maybe the next one."

Johnny scratched his head. "If it's the price, I'm sure you can get a deal and knock a few thousand off."

"It's not the price. I just don't get the right feel for the place. We'll be in touch." I grabbed Zach's hand and staggered out of the garden and back to the cars with the dogs running alongside me.

A grumpy ghost was definitely a deal-breaker. We'd just have to keep on looking for our dream home.

Chapter 16

I met Helen for breakfast the next morning in the kitchen and updated her about the latest house hunting disaster.

"We'll keep looking until everyone's happy," she said as she smothered her toast with raspberry preserves. "I don't want you compromising on where we're going to live. If there are ghosts in a house that bother you, then they bother me. We'll find something that suits both of us. The boys will just have to be patient, or get lost."

"You're telling me to get rid of Zach if he doesn't agree with where we're going to live?"

"Keep him if you must." Helen grinned. "I don't mind Zach. But I'd be more than happy for Gunner to take a flying leap."

"Speaking of Gunner, Zach mentioned that he's been asking about you."

"What's he been asking?" Her blue eyes widened. "I can't imagine why he's interested in me."

I returned her wide-eyed look of innocence. "I can't imagine what he sees in you either. All that big blonde hair and those gorgeous curves. It's enough to make a man feel queasy."

Helen smacked my hand. "You're just being silly. Gunner's not my type, and I'm not his."

I ate my toast as I studied her. I'd never seen Helen like this around a guy before. She was quick to fall head over heels in love, but it burnt out quickly and she'd find some small reason to get rid of the guy before it got serious.

Her feelings for Gunner seemed different. There was a definite spark every time the two of them met, but they were denying it. Well, maybe Gunner wasn't denying it, but Helen was fighting this so hard that it made me think this time her feelings could be genuine.

"Gunner likes you. Maybe you should consider him. Perhaps go out on a date and see how you get on away from the stress of house hunting."

Helen placed her toast down. "He's only teasing me. I'm just a challenge to Gunner. I can always tell when a man's being honest with me."

"Is that why you went out with a secret cross-dresser who assisted in covering up two murders not so long ago?"

"Even you were fooled into thinking Henry was a decent guy." Helen glared at me. "And as soon as I saw him investigating my shoes, I knew something was off with him."

"All I'm saying is give Gunner a chance. You might be surprised."

"Enough talk about the annoying Gunner," Helen said. "I heard Lady Cordelia complaining that you were missing yesterday. What were you up to?"

I gave her a quick run-down on my failed attempt to find the new will. "And you're not going to believe this, but Sebastien has a boyfriend and is trying to con money out of Lady Cordelia. He also thinks she may have killed Leo."

Helen's jaw dropped open. "I knew their relationship was strange. And Sebastien's so well-dressed and smart."

"Meaning what?"

"Just that gay guys have a sense of style that men like Zach often fall down on."

"Zach has great style," I said.

"He pulls off the casual and crumpled gardener look well," she said. "But he could learn a thing or two from Sebastien. And Sebastien commented on how nice my dress was when we met. I should have picked up on that."

"Stop with the stereotypes about gay guys," I said. "Anyway, I agreed not to tell Lady Cordelia what he's been up to, so long as Sebastien lets her down gently and doesn't steal from her. In return, he's helping me investigate what went on with Leo."

"It'll be handy to have someone on the inside," Helen said. "All we're finding so far are more suspects and no real clues."

I nodded, and was just contemplating a second round of toast when I heard raised voices outside. I jumped up and looked out the window.

"What's going on?" Helen asked.

"I'm not sure. That sounds like Lady Cordelia. Let's go take a look."

We hurried outside and discovered Lady Cordelia standing next to her black Bentley. Her face was bright red and her hands were on her hips. Spray painted on the side of the car were the words *cat killer* in shaky bright-green paint.

A police car was in the driveway. Nell stood by the car, her hands cuffed behind her back.

I glanced at Helen, and she shrugged. We stopped a short distance away.

"It has to be her. She threatened me just the other day. And now this." Lady Cordelia jabbed a finger at the damaged car. "Who knows what she might do next. My life could be at risk if she's not locked away."

"We'll take Nell in for questioning," one of the police officers said. "And we'll keep you informed as to what we discover."

"I told you to leave the estate." Lady Cordelia glared at Nell. "You aren't welcome here. I'll have a restraining order put on you if I have to. You're not to step foot on my land or in my property again. And you are never going to see any of those cats again either."

Nell returned Lady Cordelia's glare. "I knew you hated the cats. You want to have them killed. Sandy told me what your plans are."

"You don't know what you're talking about," Lady Cordelia said. "And what I decide to do with those animals is my business. You no longer work here."

"Because you unfairly sacked me," Nell said.

"I can't deal with this." Lady Cordelia waved a hand at the police officers. "Take her away."

The police officers exchanged an amused glance, before one of them encouraged Nell into the back of the police car.

"What's going on?" I asked Lady Cordelia as I walked closer with Helen by my side.

"I'm getting rid of a problem." Lady Cordelia watched the police car being driven away before turning to me, her expression cold enough to freeze my blood. "And none of this would have happened if you'd gotten rid of those cats like I asked you to. Nell keeps coming back despite me insisting she leaves. No matter how many times I tell her she's fired, she turns up to feed and clean out the cats. And now she's done this." She pointed at the car again.

I sent up a silent cheer, impressed at Nell's determination to ensure the cats didn't suffer.

"Did you see her do it?" Helen asked.

"No, but who else would it be?" Lady Cordelia said. "She's getting petty revenge because she lost her job."

"Maybe some of the other staff on the estate are also unhappy that the cats are going," I said. "People like them being around. They'll be missed."

"I don't care if they'll be missed," Lady Cordelia said. "This is your fault, Lorna."

"I'm doing what I can to find homes for the cats." There was no way I was taking the blame for Nell getting handy with a tin of paint.

"You need to work faster and more efficiently," Lady Cordelia said. "I want those cats gone by the end of the week, or you'll need to find yourself a new job."

Tabitha ran out of the house, wearing a pair of silky pink pajamas. "What's going on? Did I see a police car take Nell away?"

"There's nothing to worry yourself about that," Lady Cordelia said. "Nell's got herself into a bit of trouble. She won't be back here again."

"What did she do?" Tabitha smoothed her bed-messy blonde hair down over her bandaged head.

"Ruined the Bentley." Lady Cordelia gave a sigh. "Go inside Tabitha. You're not presentable to be seen in public."

"Who will look after the cats if Nell's gone?" she asked. "Our little fur balls need someone to keep them well-groomed."

"They'll be gone soon enough," Lady Cordelia said. "That won't be our responsibility."

"Nell was always so good with the cats," Tabitha said. "And she let me play with the kittens."

"Get inside and put some clothes on," Lady Cordelia snapped. "It's not decent to be seen outside in your nightwear."

Tabitha stared at the spray paint on the car before shrugging and turning back toward the castle. As she did so, I spotted Julius and Montgomery standing by the front door. Both were dressed as if they'd come in from a posh night out, and wore crumpled tuxedos, their bow ties hanging loosely around their necks. They were huddled together and looked deep in conversation.

Seeing Julius again reminded me that I needed to find out more about his plans for the animal park and just how determined he was to make it happen.

Everyone else slowly dispersed, and I was just going back to the house with Helen and Flipper when Sandy ran up. "I just heard Nell was arrested."

"Lady Cordelia think she vandalized her car," I said, gesturing to the Bentley.

Sandy's eyebrows shot up. "She does have a fiery temper, and she was furious when Lady Cordelia banned her from coming to see the cats. I'm not sure she'd do anything like that, though."

"Lady Cordelia is convinced it was her," Helen said.

"Are you going to be all right at the animal sanctuary on your own?" I asked Sandy. "That's a lot of cats to take care of."

"I'll have to work late until I get everything done," Sandy said. "It's not fair the cats miss out because Lady Cordelia's firing anyone who says a bad word about her."

"I'll come and give you a hand on my lunch break," I said.

"I'd appreciate that," Sandy said. "Fifty litter trays don't get emptied on their own."

I wrinkled my nose but nodded. "I'll meet up with you later. We can tackle those litter boxes together." I looked over to where Julius had been standing, hoping I'd be able to have a word with him, but he'd vanished along with Montgomery.

My interrogation would have to wait.

I grabbed a quick sandwich from the kitchen at lunchtime, before heading to the cat sanctuary to give Sandy a hand with the feeding and cleaning, and hopefully tickling lots of cute cats.

She waved as she saw me round the corner and gestured me over.

"I'm glad you could make it. I fed them all at breakfast, but there's still plenty to do." Sandy passed me a plastic apron and pointed at a pair of green welly boots. "It's best to put those on. You need to make sure your shoes are free from germs so you don't spread any infections around."

"You must be missing Nell," I said as I tied the apron around my middle and shoved my feet in the boots.

"Like you wouldn't believe," Sandy said. "I've never known anybody work harder than her. She was devoted to the cats. I still can't believe she's been fired. And now Lady Cordelia's had her arrested. It's not fair."

"You really don't think she vandalized Lady Cordelia's car?" I took the broom Sandy held out for me.

"I wouldn't have said she's that spiteful, but it's possible," Sandy said. "She loves cats more than people. And with Lady Cordelia insisting on getting rid of them, I can't say I blame Nell for letting her anger take over."

"Maybe when Lady Cordelia calms down she'll have a change of heart about Nell." I followed Sandy along a row of cat houses, slowing occasionally to tickle the chin of a waiting cat.

"I shouldn't think she will," Sandy said. "Lady Cordelia is determined to get rid of the sanctuary and us as well. I've been looking around for another job, but no luck so far. Come on, we'll work our way along this row first."

She let me into an animal house. Three timid little black faces peered out at me from the indoor enclosure. I knelt and beckoned the cats to me. "What do you think about Julius's idea for an animal park?"

"Not much," Sandy said. "And I don't know why he'd want such a thing. He doesn't even like animals. The last time he came to visit the sanctuary with Leo he complained nonstop about having allergies and said his face swelled up. If the cats do that to him, imagine what a lion will do."

"He thinks it's going to make money for the estate," I said, lowering my voice as one of the black cats crept closer, its nose snitching as it inhaled my scent.

"I get the impression young Julius is trying to make a name for himself," Sandy said as she emptied litter trays and changed the water in the cats' bowls. "He was always presenting some wild idea or other to his father. None of them were taken seriously. Julius needs to take a vacation, get a girlfriend, and stop worrying about his reputation. He can get stressed when he's middle-aged, has a pot belly, and high blood pressure."

"If he offered you a job in the animal park, would you take it?"

Sandy looked over and shrugged. "Beggars can't be choosers, but I wouldn't be happy about it. I'm not even sure keeping wild animals in a place like this is right. Imagine if one of them got into the castle when it was full of visitors? It's a big responsibility to have such dangerous animals in the park. We even get complaints occasionally from visitors when one of the cats scratches them. Think of the compensation claims if a lion got loose and decided to take a bite out of somebody."

I grimaced as I imagined the front page news stories. It wouldn't do any good to the estate's income if something like that happened.

I finally managed to coax the cats out and gave them all a stroke before cleaning their enclosure.

We were just about to start on the next pen, when Big Ginge strolled up, his tail flicking lazily in the air as he sidled along the outside of the houses.

"Here comes trouble," Sandy said as she spotted Big Ginge.

"He does like to make himself at home," I said. "My first day here, I found him asleep on my bed."

"You'd better be careful if he's taken a liking to your bed," Sandy said. "He's the cat who was found asleep on Leo's face."

My eyebrows shot up. "Big Ginge suffocated Leo?"

Big Ginge narrowed his eyes at me and hissed.

"That's what Lady Cordelia reckons," Sandy said. "He was the only cat in the room when Leo's body was discovered."

Big Ginge hissed again and his fur bushed up.

"He doesn't seem happy about being accused of killing Leo," I said.

"That's one clever cat," Sandy said. "We used to have him in a pen, but he kept escaping. No matter what we did or how many locks we put on the door, he'd always get out. He's like the Harry Houdini of cats. But he was Leo's favorite, which is why he got to sleep in his bedroom. It's a shame their friendship had such a sad ending."

I stepped outside the cat house and tried to give Big Ginge a stroke, but he backed away from me, his ears low and his eyes wide. He was definitely unhappy about being accused of smothering Leo.

"Let's go. Plenty more cats to clean out." Sandy unlocked the next house and ushered me in.

I stepped inside and began cleaning, but paused and watched as Big Ginge strolled away. Big Ginge was innocent and I was getting more interested in Julius as Leo's killer.

It was time to pin down the prodigal son and see what secrets he was hiding.

Chapter 17

After helping Sandy clean out the rest of the cat houses, I was in need of a shower, but didn't dare take the time off until I'd finished working with Lady Cordelia.

She'd barely spoken to me all morning, and the atmosphere between us was frosty. I still hadn't forgiven her for complaining about me to Sebastien. And from the way she was giving me the cold shoulder, she was equally unimpressed by me.

I was glad when she curtly dismissed me at the end of the day. I hurried to my room to take a quick shower before dinner.

I was just scrubbing the smell of litter trays off me when Leo's head popped around the shower curtain.

"Get out of here!" I hurled my loofah at him. "No ghosts in the shower."

Leo ducked his head back and vanished.

I grumbled under my breath as I swiftly washed the conditioner out of my hair. That was one rule I had when it came to ghosts; they didn't disturb me when I was in the shower. No pervy ghosts allowed.

I groped around for a towel and wrapped it around my body, before stepping out of the shower.

Leo was still in the bathroom, but had his back to me and his face to the wall.

I swiftly wrapped a pink fluffy towel around my hair. "I'm decent now. Next time, wait until I'm out of the shower before making your presence known."

Leo turned around slowly, a sorrowful look on his face as he kept his eyes on the floor.

"I still haven't figured out who killed you," I said as I wiped steam off the bathroom mirror. "But I am interested in Julius."

Leo shrugged and shook his head.

I massaged cream into my face. "Do you know Julius is going ahead with his wild animal park? Everyone I've talked to has told me you were dead set against the idea. I'm thinking he decided to get you out of the way so he could carry on with his plan."

Leo shrugged again, not seeming enthused by my idea.

"Wait for me in the kitchen," I said. "I need to get dressed, and you're definitely not watching that. Perhaps we can come up with some useful information if we spend time considering each suspect."

Leo nodded and vanished from sight.

I still waited a few seconds before dropping my towel, not wanting him to unexpectedly arrive when I was naked.

I dressed in my favorite pair of soft gray trousers and a black pullover, before swiftly drying my hair, and then headed to the kitchen with Flipper to see what Helen had cooked us for dinner.

As I walked through the doorway, I could hear Helen talking.

I spotted Leo drifting around in one corner and Big Ginge perched on a seat by the table, his gaze intent on Helen as she cooked.

"Talking to yourself is the first sign of madness, you know." I sat at the table and grabbed a hunk of warm homemade bread from the plate in front of me.

Helen brandished a wooden spoon at me. "I'm not alone. I know Leo's here because I've been shivering for several minutes. We also have a four-legged guest. He's interested in everything I have to tell him." She gestured to Big Ginge who was washing himself and rubbing his paw over his ears.

"Am I forgiven yet?" I asked him.

Big Ginge paused from his washing and regarded me with large bright eyes.

"What did you do to him?" Helen asked.

"I was with Sandy at lunchtime," I said. "She reckons Big Ginge was the cat who suffocated Leo. Big Ginge thinks otherwise."

Leo rushed over to the table and spun around it several times, shaking his hand and rattling the cutlery.

"And from the way Leo's behaving, he also doesn't agree with that theory." I gripped the edge of the table as I waited for the dizziness to pass.

Flipper began chasing after Leo and snapping at him.

"Whatever Leo's doing tell him to stop," Helen said. "The kitchen feels like we're in a freezer. If I get too dizzy I won't be able to finish dinner."

"You heard the lady," I said to Leo. "You need to calm down so we can discuss what's going on."

Leo stopped by Big Ginge and pointed at him before shaking his head. Flipper ran straight through Leo and then turned and jumped up at him.

"I get that you don't think Big Ginge had anything to do with your death," I said as I patted Flipper's head to calm him.

"The newspaper reports suggests otherwise." Helen sat at the table.

"What do you know?" I asked.

"I've been doing a bit of research," she said. "I looked up the media reports on Leo's death. It turns out he had cat fur lodged in his throat. That's why they believe a cat suffocated him in his sleep. And it was ginger fur they found."

Big Ginge narrowed his eyes at Helen as if he understood what she was saying.

"Be careful what you say next," I cautioned her. "Big Ginge is not amused."

Helen shot the cat a cautious look. "The newspapers also reported that swabs of Leo's skin were taken and they found cat saliva on his face."

"That does seem like damning evidence," I said, my attention still on Big Ginge.

Big Ginge shook himself and a cloud of fur floated from his body.

"You see!" Helen pointed at the fur. "And he's a big cat. It wouldn't be difficult for him to curl up on Leo's face and suffocate him."

Big Ginge growled.

"Even if you didn't mean to," Helen said swiftly.

I wished Big Ginge could talk and tell us what really happened.

The kitchen door banged open. Sebastien hurried in, glancing furtively over his shoulder. "I'm glad you're here." He looked at Helen and raised his eyebrows at me. "Is it okay if we talk about you know what?"

"Helen knows everything," I said. "Sit down, we were just about to eat dinner if you want to join us."

"No thanks, but I found something that might be interesting," Sebastien said.

"Is it the will?" I asked.

"No, but it's got something to do with Julius and this park idea," Sebastien said. "I haven't got long. Lady Cordelia is on the hunt for me. She wants us to have a romantic dinner out." He grimaced.

"Remember what I said. Be nice to her." Not that I thought she deserved it anymore, not after the way she'd treated me today.

"I'm doing my best," Sebastien said. "She'd try the patience of a saint."

"What did you find out?" Helen asked.

"It's a big loan Julius wants to take out." Sebastien pulled out several sheets of paper from his inside jacket pocket and handed them to me.

I read through the paperwork quickly. "Julius wants to re-mortgage the castle for millions and gamble it on this wild animal park idea."

Leo spun up to the ceiling and flew around the table several times.

Sebastien grabbed the back of a chair as the color leached from his skin. "Is anyone else feeling giddy?"

Leo knocked over the condiments on the table, his face livid as he shot past me again. Someone was not happy with Julius's loan idea.

"Why don't you sit down?" Helen jumped up and grabbed the condiments, setting them upright. "Maybe you're feeling lightheaded because you haven't had any dinner."

Sebastien nodded and fumbled his way into a seat before putting his head in his hands. "I get these strange feelings sometimes when I'm in the castle. It's like everything's tilting. And I've walked through plenty of cold spots when I've been here. That's supposed to be a sign ghosts are around, isn't it? Do you think the rumors about this place being haunted are true?"

I looked at Leo who was still spinning around the kitchen. "It's possible."

"I'm open-minded to the idea of ghosts," Sebastien said. "I had a great aunt who used to be able to read people's futures from their tea leaves. She'd brew a disgustingly strong batch of tea, make you drink it down and then spill the remains of the cup into a saucer. Then she'd predict what was going to happen to you. I was never sure if I believed her, but she did tell me that she saw me living in a castle. Maybe there is something to that sort of thing."

I gestured at Leo to slow down, and after another spin around the room he stopped by my chair and glared at me.

"This loan agreement gives Julius a strong motive for killing Leo," I said.

"You need to be careful," Sebastien said. "He's your employer's son. He could have you sacked. I know he's made up stories about other members of staff he didn't like so he could get rid of them. Cordelia always sides with Julius, so you won't stand a chance if he wants you gone."

"And she's already looking for an excuse to fire me," I said.

"Is there any way we can ask Julius about it discreetly?" Helen said.

"Would you be prepared to use your amazing flirting techniques on him?" I asked. "You could get something useful out of Julius if you smiled sweetly enough."

"Not this time," Helen said. "I'm rationing my flirting to men I consider serious husband material."

"And you won't get that with Julius," Sebastien said. "He's is too busy trying to be the boss of this place to notice you. Not that you aren't lovely."

Helen smoothed down her hair. "Thank you for noticing."

"Is your hair color natural?" he asked. "It's so shiny. You must use a treatment on it."

"It's all mine," Helen said. "The color and the shine."

"Let's talk about hair dye another time," I said. "We need to figure out a way to get Julius to open up about this loan and find out what he told Leo about his plans to re-mortgage the castle."

Leo jabbed a finger at the loan paperwork and shook his head.

"It could be that Leo was in the dark about the loan. Julius was going behind his back," I said, more for Leo's consideration than anyone else's.

Leo nodded along with my theorizing.

"And if Julius became suspicious that his father was on to him and didn't want him to stop the loan going through, he may have needed to act hastily."

Leo tilted his head to one side and frowned.

Sebastien groaned and raised a hand. "Very well. I'll be your sacrificial lamb."

"What do you mean?" I asked.

"I simply can't stand being mauled by Cordelia anymore. And since I'm not going to get any money out of this, I need to bring it to a halt. I'll confront Julius with what we've found out and see what he's prepared to tell me. I can use this as my way to escape from Cordelia, and maybe even help Leo at the same time."

"Julius isn't a fan of yours," I said. "We saw that over dinner the other night. He might not tell you anything."

"I've always made it clear to him that I thought he wasn't mature enough to run this estate. He's never forgiven me for that," Sebastien said. "Confronting him about this loan will only enrage him further. If I upset Julius enough, Cordelia will side with him and fall out with me. It's the excuse I need to get out of here."

I raised my eyebrows and nodded. Sebastien had an ulterior motive for confronting Julius but it worked in our favor. And if he could find out what we needed, I was prepared to offer him up as our sacrifice. "Okay, then we need to make a plan to get you and Julius in the same room and find out what he knows."

"And we need to do it quickly," Sebastien said. "If I have to spend one more night fending off Cordelia's advances, there might be another murder to investigate."

Chapter 18

I disinfected my hands before leaving the cat houses. I'd spent an hour with Sandy after work helping her tidy everything. She was still struggling on her own, and Lady Cordelia wasn't being any help and simply kept saying the cats would be taken away soon, so Sandy didn't need extra assistance.

I hurried back to the castle with Flipper to find Helen already waiting for me outside the gatehouse.

"You're late." She grabbed my elbow and hurried me around the side of the castle.

"You can't hurry a cat when they won't eat their dinner," I said.

"Sebastien is already on his way to see Julius," Helen said. "We don't want to miss what he has to say."

Sebastien had convinced Julius to meet with him that evening and discuss a fictitious business opportunity. They were meeting in a downstairs study so we'd be able to listen in through the window.

Big Ginge came running out from a hedge and ran alongside Flipper as we neared the window.

"Not a word out of either of you," I said to Flipper and Big Ginge. "We need to be discreet."

Both animals looked up at me with big innocent eyes.

As we reached the window, I could hear the sound of a quiet male voice.

Helen risked a look through the window and then ducked back. "Julius is in there on his phone. And he's got one leg in plaster!"

"That's odd. He was fine when I saw him this morning. I wonder what he's done." I was about to take a look myself, when there was a knock at the door.

We listened as Julius finished his phone call.

The knock sounded again, this time louder.

"Enter," Julius said, his tone already sounding irritated.

"Julius, how are you?" It was Sebastien, and he sounded nervous. "Oh! You've hurt your leg."

"Well spotted. I'm busy," Julius said. "What did you want to talk to me about? You said something about a business opportunity. I've already got a lot going on right now, so I can't take on too much additional work."

"Yes, I imagine you have with your plans for the animal park," Sebastien said.

There was a short pause. "What do you know about that?"

There was the rustling of paper and I exchanged a glance with Helen. Sebastien must be showing Julius the loan papers he'd discovered.

"I found some interesting information about how you're raising the finance for your park," Sebastien said.

The silence lasted for so long that I couldn't help but look in the window. Julius was staring at the papers Sebastien had laid on the table. Two bright-red spots of color were on his cheeks and he was grinding his teeth together.

"This is none of your business," Julius said, his tone low and threatening.

"I'm making it my business," Sebastien said. "Does Cordelia know about this loan?"

"What my mother knows is also none of your concern," Julius said. "You're her plaything. A toy she's already getting tired of you."

I looked down to see Flipper and Big Ginge listening into the conversation, their heads cocked to one side. Big Ginge was nestled between Flipper's paws.

"My relationship with your mother is none of your business," Sebastien said. "But it does worry me that you might be taking advantage of her."

"You'd know all about that," Julius said. "I know you're not here because you love her."

"I do care for your mother," Sebastien said. "And I care that you might be abusing your position as her son."

"Very well. How much do you want?" Julius asked.

"Excuse me?"

"If you pretend you've never seen this paperwork and suddenly decide you have to leave on urgent business and never come back, how much money would it take to make that happen?"

I opened my mouth and stared at Helen. I hadn't expected Julius to bribe Sebastien. I knew how desperate he was for money so he could start his new life with Elton. This could ruin our plans.

Sebastien made a few garbled-sounding noises before clearing his throat. "It's not about money."

I let out a relieved sigh, glad Sebastien wasn't going to cave in.

"You'll have your price," Julius said. "You must have, otherwise why would you be with my mother?"

"It's not right that you're going to re-mortgage the castle without her knowing," Sebastien said. "This is her home."

"And it's not right you're dating a woman twice your age," Julius said. "It seems that both of us have gotten a few things wrong."

"I only want what's right for Cordelia," Sebastien said. "And you selling this castle out from under her isn't it."

"She won't lose a thing," Julius said. "The investment is sound. The new park will pay for itself within five years. All I need is this initial investment. Once I have it, the work can begin. I have everything planned out. You're not going to get in my way."

"I could stop you if I told Cordelia what I've found out," Sebastien said.

"She won't believe you if you go telling tales about me," Julius said.

"Why do you think Cordelia is still running the estate?" Sebastien asked. "She doesn't trust you to do a good job with the existing business. Do you really think she's going to let you loose on turning the grounds into some free-for-all that's full of bears and elephants?"

"I'm not having bears." Julius's tone was sulky.

"Your mother thinks you're a joke," Sebastien said. "And she'll think that even more when she discovers what you're trying to do. You'll have to get her to sign off on this loan. She'll never agree to that."

I bit my bottom lip as their voices raised. This wasn't going how I'd planned. They weren't supposed to be trading insults. Sebastien should be asking Julius about Leo and what he knew about the loan for the park.

"Maybe we need to intervene," Helen whispered.

"Give Sebastien one more minute. He might be trying to rile Julius up so he makes a mistake and confesses."

"Why don't we get Mommy in here and see what she has to say about this?" Julius asked. "And she'll be interested to hear that you accepted money from me to disappear."

"I did no such thing you little snake," Sebastien said. "I should have done, though. This family is a nightmare. What you're doing is wrong and I want that straightened out."

"You haven't been straight with us since you stepped through the front door," Julius said. "I see the way you covet things around you and wish you'd been born into such wealth. It won't be the same if you do marry my mother. She won't give you what you want. She'll keep you on a tight leash to make sure you do everything she expects of you. If you don't, the money will be cut off. And, when your looks begin to fade, she'll find another replacement. You're not that important to her."

"That's not how our relationship works," Sebastien muttered.

"Ha! Of course it is. You wouldn't be with her if she was poor."

I let out a sigh. This definitely wasn't going in the right direction. Julius had the upper hand and was now interrogating Sebastien.

"Cordelia's a nice person," Sebastien said. "If she was poor, I wouldn't care. So long as we were both happy."

Julius laughed quietly. "Of course you would. So, I'll ask you again. How much is it going to take for you to keep your big mouth shut and leave this place for good?"

I closed my eyes, sending out a wish in the hope Sebastien wasn't going to give in.

"Half a million," Sebastien said quietly.

I gasped and jumped up, but Helen pulled me down. "You'll be seen if you're not careful."

"Didn't you hear him? Sebastien's going to accept a bribe."

Julius laughed again. "I knew you were only in this relationship for the money. Now I have your words recorded on my phone, I'm going to let Mommy know all about it. You're not going to get anything from us."

"You little sneak," Sebastien growled. "Give me your phone."

There were sounds of scuffling and a startled yelp came from Julius.

I looked through the window. Sebastien held Julius in a headlock.

I grabbed hold of the window ledge and hauled myself through. "Stop fighting you two." I caught hold of Sebastien's shoulder and tried to pull him away from Julius but he clung on tightly.

"He tricked me," Sebastien said, his normally neat hair sticking up. "He recorded our whole conversation."

"I know that," I said. "But you can't choke the information we need out of him."

"I'll give it a good go," Sebastien said. "Search his pockets and get his phone off him."

"Let me go!" Julius yelled. "I'll have you arrested." He smacked his hands against Sebastien's arm.

"Not if I throttle you first." Sebastien reached inside Julius's jacket and grabbed the phone, before stamping on it. "Now your evidence is gone."

"You'd better let Julius go," I said to Sebastien. "He's already injured. You don't want to make things any worse."

"I can still tell Mommy that you were willing to accept money from me," Julius choked out. "She'll believe me over you."

"You need air in your lungs in order to do that," Sebastien said.

Helen jumped through the window and fell on the floor. "What did I miss?"

"Just a couple of idiots," I said, before turning back to Sebastien. "No one's choking anybody. And no one's going to tell tales to their mommy."

"He deceived me!" Sebastien said.

"And you were trying to do the same to him," I said. "We all were."

"What are you talking about?" Julius's eyes bulged in his head as he stared at me.

"Let him go," I said to Sebastien. "You've destroyed the evidence. He can't do you any harm."

Sebastien released his hold on Julius. He fell to the floor, his hand around his neck as he gasped in air. "You could have killed me you madman."

"Like you did your father," Sebastien said.

Flipper and Big Ginge leaped through the window together. Big Ginge careened across the room and landed on top of Julius, making him grunt as he squashed the air out of his lungs.

Flipper charged after Big Ginge, only just missing Julius by leaping over him at the last second, causing him to cower and yelp.

"What are these crazy animals doing in here?" Julius pushed Big Ginge off his stomach and sat up. "Has everyone lost their mind? And what are you talking about, me killing my father?"

Big Ginge hopped nimbly onto the desk and curled his tail around him, his gaze going around the room as he took in the scene before him.

Flipper sat on the floor next to him and gave me a doggy smile.

"Tell us about your loan arrangement," I said to Julius. "Did Leo stop you from doing it so you decided to get rid of him?"

"You're all crazy." Julius staggered to his feet and continued to rub his neck. He leaned on the desk.

Big Ginge swiped a paw at him, making Julius jump away and land on his leg cast. He yelped and his face drained of color.

I grabbed a chair and offered it to him, seeing the pain etched on his face. "What happened to your leg?"

Julius slumped into the seat without a word of thanks. "One of the work's vehicles went out of control this morning. I was lucky not to be crushed to death under the wheels. It must have been dodgy brakes. No one was in the vehicle. It's only a fracture, so the hospital patched me up with this splint and a cast and sent me home. I'll be in this cast for three months."

I wondered if one of the workmen hadn't deliberately released the handbrake on the vehicle after Julius had been so rude to them the other day. "Getting back to the loan, I know Leo wasn't happy about what you wanted to do."

Julius shrugged. "He was old-fashioned and set in his ways. Of course he wasn't happy, but he understood a good business plan. I'd have talked him round if I'd had the opportunity to do so. But that wretched cat killed him before I got the chance."

"Or you did," Sebastien muttered.

"I didn't touch him." Julius glowered at Sebastien. "I liked him. In truth, he didn't care that much about me to be invested in what I was doing. Now he's gone, I'm just getting on with things, and making the best of it." He looked at the floor.

For a second, I felt sympathy for Julius. It must be hard to be second best to a bunch of stray cats.

"He can't have agreed to this loan you want," I said. "It would have been too much of a risk for the castle. If it goes wrong, you lose everything."

"As long as the cat sanctuary got to stay, he wouldn't have minded," Julius said. "We talked about it a few times. I could see he was warming to the idea. I got the paperwork drawn up and was going to talk him through it step-by-step, showing the repayments and the expected return on investment. It isn't a high-risk deal."

"So, why did you bribe me to get me out of the picture?" Sebastien asked. "Why the secrecy over this paperwork if it isn't a problem?"

"You're a separate problem to this." Julius glared at Sebastien. "I want you off the estate. You put ridiculous ideas in my mother's head. Just last night, she was talking about opening a section of the castle as an artists' retreat. I wonder where she got that idea from."

I also glared at Sebastien. "You didn't mention that to me. And another thing, were you serious about taking the bribe Julius offered?"

"I was briefly tempted," he said. "And the ideas I'm offering Cordelia aren't stupid. I think an artists' retreat would make a decent amount of money for the castle. Bring in a different audience."

"Artists won't bring in money," Julius said. "Most of them are poor."

Sebastien shrugged and glanced at me with a guilty look on his face.

Julius looked around the room at us all. "If you're trying to pin my father's death on anyone, it's not me you should be looking at, especially not if you think this loan for the animal park has anything to do with it."

"You mean other people are involved with your plans?" I asked.

"Sure. Tabitha and Uncle Monty also want the animal park," Julius said. "If you're going to accuse me of killing my father so the park can go ahead, you need to ask them what they're getting out of this. And they're both much more ruthless than I am."

Chapter 19

"Hold on a minute. You're all involved in getting this park up and running?" I leaned against the sofa in the study and rubbed my forehead.

"That's right," Julius said. "Uncle Monty is always hard up for money, and Tabitha doesn't care where the money comes from so long as there's lots of it to spend. They all have a stake in the castle as part of our trust agreements. We agreed to use it as collateral so we could secure the loan."

"Which means that any one of you could have killed Leo," Helen said.

Julius expression became cautious. "You're mistaken about how my father died. It was bad luck that he was smothered, wasn't it? Why do you keep saying he was killed?"

"We're not so sure his death was an accident," Sebastien said. "Lorna thinks Leo might have been murdered."

Julius turned to me. "What makes you believe that?"

"Because he was worth a lot more dead than alive," I said.

Julius shook his head. "He may not have cared for me all that much, but he was still my father. I loved him. I wouldn't want to kill him."

"What about Tabitha?" I asked, recalling how Leo had smelt flowery perfume just before he died.

Julius considered my question, his hand idly rubbing the cast on his leg. "She can be... cruel."

"Cruel how?" Helen asked. "What does she do?"

"You always hear about those odd kids who enjoy setting fire to ants' nests or pulling the wings off butterflies for fun," Julius said.

"Your sister does that?" I asked.

"She did. Now, she's graduated to cats."

My mouth fell open. "Tabitha hurts the cats in the sanctuary?"

"She told me she only takes the sick ones. The ones too ill to recover," Julius said with a shudder. "Honestly, she creeps me out. She has their fur made into slippers and collars for her clothes. She's always stroking the fur on her outfits and talking to it as if it's a living animal. And have you noticed how she stares at the cats whenever they're around? It's as if she's sizing them up to see if their fur will match her next outfit?"

"Did Leo know about this?" I swallowed my horror.

"Of course not," Julius said. "He thought she loved the cats. And I guess she does in her own twisted little way. She loves what they can give her. She's not right in the head."

My hand went to Flipper's head and I gave him a stroke, more to reassure myself than him. "Tabitha needs serious help."

"That's so disturbing," Helen said. "And it doesn't take much of a leap for her to go from killing cats to killing her father."

"Well, it's a bit of a stretch," Sebastien said. "But I agree, it is creepy."

It made sense now why the cats ran from Tabitha whenever she tried to get near them. They probably knew she was considering them for her next pair of mittens. "Did you know that Leo was planning to change his will?" I asked Julius.

"He'd mentioned it to me," he said. "I never saw any new will, though. It was the same old one he'd always talked about when the details were read out. He'd always planned to leave money in trust for me and Tabitha, the main estate to Mommy, and some donations to various charities. It was nothing out of the ordinary."

"He also planned to leave money to a close friend," I said. "Do you know who that would be?"

"Father's only friends were the cats," Julius said. "I suppose you're going to tell me he planned to leave everything to them?"

Tabitha strolled through the doorway of the study, wrapped in a long fur-trimmed shawl. She paused as she saw us all. "This looks interesting. What are you all doing?"

"I'm glad you're here," I said, failing not to shudder as I saw the fur on her shawl.

Tabitha took a step back and glared at me. "What do you want? I don't have any filing if you're looking for extra work. Although I hear you've been enjoying yourself with the kitty litter. Mommy's thinking of moving you over to temporary pooper scooper since you can't do the work she's instructed you to do."

"They know about the park loan." Julius sighed. "You may as well come in. They also know that you're involved."

"I don't have time to discuss boring loans." Tabitha waved her hand dismissively. "I was looking for Uncle

Monty. He promised to take me for dinner, and I'm getting hungry."

"Dinner will have to wait," I said.

Tabitha's nostrils flared. "How dare you talk to me like that."

I eyed the fur on her shawl again and grimaced. "Nice outfit. Where did you get it from?"

"Somewhere you'd never be able to afford," Tabitha sneered.

"They think someone killed our father," Julius said.

Tabitha blinked several times and grabbed hold of the door. "Whatever makes you think that?"

"Do you know anything about it?" I asked her.

"You think I did it?" she asked, a scowl creasing her face.

"You do have a lot to gain by him being dead," Julius said.

Tabitha trailed her fingers across the fur on her shawl. "If I had anything to gain by Daddy's death, then so did you. Why not blame my brother for this?"

"Maybe it's time we get the police involved," Helen said.

"There's no need for that. You'd be wasting their time. Daddy's death was an accident." Tabitha backed away, a panicked look crossing her face.

"Tell us what you know," I said.

"What are you talking about? I don't know anything!"

"You should confess if you've done something stupid," Julius said. "We'll find out in the end."

I looked at Julius in surprise. It appeared we were on the same side.

"So should you." Tabitha narrowed her eyes at Julius. "I wish that lorry had run over your head and not just your leg."

"Then you would have inherited my money." Julius struggled to his feet, waving away Sebastien's offer of a hand up. "You do know something about Father's death, don't you? What did you do to him?"

"What rubbish," Tabitha said. "I had nothing to do with it. A cat sat on his stupid face. You think I trained a cat to do that?"

"Tabitha, we only want to help you," I said. "If you got angry and lashed out at Leo, the police will understand."

Her gaze shot around the room. "Stop ganging up on me. I had nothing to do with it." Tabitha wobbled on her black heels, before turning and running out of the room.

"Don't let her get away." I dashed after Tabitha, along the hallway and to the front door, closing on her with every step. There was a lot to be said for preferring practical pumps over high heels.

"You stay away from me." Tabitha yanked open the door and slammed it in my face just as I reached it.

I hurried outside. Tabitha was fleeing across the gravel toward the cat sanctuary.

I whistled for Flipper and he shot out the window, closely followed by Big Ginge. They joined me as I ran across the grass after Tabitha.

I was gasping for air by the time we got to the cat houses. Tabitha was nowhere to be seen. I looked down at Flipper and Big Ginge. "Go find Tabitha for me."

Flipper set his nose to the ground and began to sniff, while Big Ginge nonchalantly strolled past all the houses, peering in at each resident as if to show off his freedom.

I crept along the rows of cat houses, trying to see if Tabitha had snuck into any of them and was hiding from us.

Flipper barked, signaling he'd found something.

I ran to join him. Tabitha was crouching in a corner by a maintenance door. "You stay away from me. Don't let your dog bite me."

"Flipper won't bite," I said. "Why did you run?"

"Because you just accused me of murder." Tabitha spun around and pulled open the door to the maintenance room.

I dashed in behind her, the door slamming shut, and ran straight into her back. "Oomph! What's the matter?"

Tabitha pointed in front of her. "It's Uncle Monty!"

I peered around Tabitha's shoulder. Montgomery was unconscious and tied to a chair.

Chapter 20

"What happened to him?" I hurried over and checked Montgomery's pulse. I let out a relieved sigh as I felt his heartbeat, and quickly untied his hands and feet.

"Who would do such a thing to him?" Tabitha asked. "We were supposed to be going to dinner."

Montgomery groaned and his eyes flickered open. "I feel like I've been kicked in the head by a horse. Who hit me?"

I gently slapped his cheek to keep him conscious. "Montgomery, it's Lorna. Do you know what happened to you?"

"I was in the garden," Montgomery said, "waiting for Tabitha. I decided to take a look at the cats. All I remember is hearing someone walking up behind me and then getting smacked on the back of the head." He moved his fingers up to his head and winced.

"You didn't see who hit you?" I asked.

He blinked slowly and gently shook his head. "Not a clue. Where am I?"

"Someone tied you up and left you in one of the maintenance rooms," I said. "Do you think you can stand?"

Montgomery took a deep breath and slowly got to his feet. I let him take hold of my arm until I was certain he wasn't going to fall over.

"Are we still going for dinner?" Tabitha asked.

I sighed and shook my head. She was surprisingly unconcerned at just having discovered her uncle knocked out and tied up. Julius was right. Tabitha was a weird one.

"Maybe another night." Montgomery patted Tabitha on the shoulder as he staggered past. "I've got a bit of a headache to deal with."

"But you promised," she said. "And I'm wearing my new fur shawl."

"In case you haven't noticed, someone just tried to kill your uncle," I said.

"He looks fine to me," she said. "You are okay, aren't you, Uncle Monty?"

"Just perfect," he sighed.

I tilted my head and looked at the bruise on Tabitha's forehead. "Remind me again what happened to you? How did you get that bruise?"

"A silly problem with the car," Tabitha said. "The brakes failed."

"And you're sure it was a fault on the car?" I said. "Has anyone checked to make sure the brakes were actually faulty?"

"I'm not sure," she said. "I never bother with that sort of thing. I left the garage and the insurance company to deal with it. Why do you want to know?"

Were the accidents that had been happening around here something more sinister? Tabitha's car running off the road and Julius being injured by a van no one was driving. "What if the brakes on your car had been tampered with?" I asked.

"You think someone is trying to bump us all off?" Montgomery laughed. "Who would want to do such a thing?"

"You've just been whacked over the head and tied up," I said. "That was no accident."

He grunted. "But who wants us all dead?"

"Yes! Why would anybody want to kill me?" Tabitha looked at Montgomery. "Uncle Monty, make this woman stop talking nonsense."

Montgomery scratched his chin. "Lorna might be onto something. It is strange how all of us have been injured recently."

I heard scrabbling at the door and opened it to find Flipper, Big Ginge, and Helen waiting outside.

"What's going on?" Helen asked. "Has Tabitha confessed to killing Leo?"

"I've confessed to nothing." Tabitha pouted and folded her arms over her chest. "That's because I'm guilty of nothing."

"Using cat fur on your clothes doesn't make you innocent in my eyes," I said coldly.

Tabitha's lips flapped open and shut a few times. "I don't know what you're talking about."

"We'll deal with that later." I turned to Helen. "We just found Montgomery tied up in here."

"Lorna thinks someone tried to kill me," Montgomery said.

Helen's eyes widened. "The broken leg, the bump on the head, and now this." She gestured at Montgomery.

"I don't feel very well." Tabitha sagged against Montgomery, and he awkwardly patted her shoulder. "All this talk of killing is ruining my appetite. I was looking forward to some juicy veal or a bloody steak."

"Everything will be okay." Montgomery looked over at me and shrugged. "Perhaps we should go back to the castle and discuss this. And I need something for my headache. Whoever hit me didn't do it gently."

Five minutes later, we were back in the study with Julius and Sebastien. Montgomery had just finished updated them as to what happened to him.

"Does anyone have any idea who would want to get rid of you all?" I looked around the room, but nobody seemed all that keen on meeting my gaze.

"Dare I mention Lady Cordelia?" Helen said.

"Mommy would never harm us." Tabitha sat stiffly on the sofa.

"She doesn't like the prospect of an animal park in the grounds," I said.

"She was coming around to the idea," Julius said.

"No, she wasn't," Sebastien said. "Cordelia complains about it all the time to me. She detests the thought of the estate being used in such a way."

"I hate to be the one to say it, but we were being reckless trying to get the animal park off the ground without Cordelia's support," Montgomery said.

"But the castle eats money," Julius said. "This is a logical step. We need to move forward and diversify the castle's business interests."

"Setting the park to one side," I said, "can any of you think of a common enemy you have? If your accidents weren't accidental and someone is trying to bump you off, who would benefit from you all being dead? Who's next in line to inherit the estate?"

Montgomery drummed his fingers against his knee and stared at the ceiling. Tabitha plucked imaginary pieces of lint from her pants, and Julius scratched his chin.

I groaned and rolled my shoulders. "There must be somebody. What about nephews and nieces, or relatives of Leo's?"

"It was just the two of us," Montgomery said. "Leo was always the sensible older brother. And as for other relatives, we're a small family. Our parents are dead. There are a couple of great aunts. They're both wealthy and wouldn't be interested in this estate."

"What about business partners?" Helen asked. "Perhaps one of them has their eye on the estate. If they can get rid of everyone who benefits from it, they might try to buy it at a bargain price."

Julius shook his head. "Father always kept business in the family. He didn't like having outsiders involved. Diversifying the park was a problem for him because I wanted to bring in outside investors."

"Which is why you killed him." Tabitha glared at Julius.

"Shut up," Julius said. "Stop trying to make people think I'm involved. You're the one with the weird urges to kill anything that has fur on it."

Helen leaned over to me. "None of this is getting us any closer to figuring out what happened to Leo."

I looked around the room again. We could be sitting with Leo's killer only a few feet away. "Leo didn't die of natural causes or by accident. And I believe all of your injuries were staged to look like mishaps. The killer is still out there."

"Apart from my injury," Montgomery said. "Someone very much intended to bash me over the head and leave me to starve in the maintenance room. Or maybe they were waiting to come back and finish me off."

"It could be that whoever hit you was going to make your death look like an accident too," Helen said. "They just didn't get the chance to after Lorna found you."

I nodded. "That's very possible. We just got lucky in getting you out of there. Somebody is trying to kill you all."

"And that someone is in this room," Sebastien said.

It was as if he'd read my thoughts. "That's also possible."

"You think I faked being run over so I wouldn't be considered a suspect in my father's death?" Julius snorted and shook his head. "Nobody killed father. He was smothered by a cat."

"Where were you all when Leo died?" I asked.

"We've already been over this with the proper authorities," Tabitha said. "I was with Julius working on the plans for the park."

"And I was out at a bar," Montgomery said. "I've got dozens of witnesses, and a rather pretty young lady who'd happily vouch for me." He raised his eyebrows and winked at me.

Sebastien shrugged. "They're right. And I was with Cordelia all evening. We had the police here questioning everybody after Leo died. After the autopsy showed the cause of death, the investigation ended. The police were convinced nothing untoward happened."

"You all need to be careful," I said. "If there is a killer on the loose, they could still be targeting you. They must have a reason for wanting all of you died. And the one thing you all have in common is this castle."

"So make sure you watch your backs," Helen said.

"I don't suppose you want to watch mine for me," Montgomery said.

"You're big enough and ugly enough to look after yourself," Helen said.

Montgomery touched his injured head. "Not this time I wasn't. I didn't see the attacker coming. I need extra protection."

"What your attack suggests is that the killer knows their way around the estate," I said. "If they can move about undetected, you've most likely seen them before and don't think it's odd that they're on the estate."

"We have dozens of staff," Tabitha said. "Along with the ones in the kitchen and the garden, we have the seasonal staff who manage the castle itself."

"And we have several dozen volunteers involved in giving castle tours," Julius said. "It could be any of them. I wouldn't expect it to be unusual to see them in the grounds. Some of them like to look around as they make up their own tour presentations. I often see strangers wandering about looking at the castle and muttering to themselves. I don't pay them any attention."

I tipped my head back. All of these potential suspects would take weeks to investigate, and I wanted Leo to get peace, and for me to get back to doing the job I was meant to. Or find a new one if Lady Cordelia got her way.

Julius and Tabitha started bickering again, and Montgomery excused himself to go lie down after his kidnapping experience.

Sebastien patted my hand. "Sorry I wasn't much help."

"You were great. Thanks for what you did."

"I'd better start getting my stuff together," he said. "When Cordelia hears about this, she's going to be fuming. The two of you need to look out as well. Julius is going to tell her everything. He won't be able to resist getting you in trouble." He turned and left the room.

I sighed and looked over at Helen. "Where shall we start? I have a bad feeling we're not going to be welcome here for much longer. And Leo still needs our help."

Helen pursed her lips as she stood. "How about we get some tea and cake? All this arguing and running around is exhausting."

We left Julius and Tabitha to their bickering. Helen was right, tea and cake always made the world look brighter, and it might give me the energy I needed to start work on all the new potential suspects.

Chapter 21

"Can you bring me through some clean newspaper for the litter trays?" Sandy shouted from the other end of the cat houses. "I'm all out down here."

I raised my hand in acknowledgement, and headed to the boxes of old newspaper kept in the store room.

It was almost the end of another day of working with the cats. After all the confrontations yesterday, I was glad when Lady Cordelia announced I was to work with Sandy in the sanctuary until further notice. Although it wasn't what I was used to doing, I liked being away from Lady Cordelia and her sarcastic remarks about my abilities.

It also gave me time to think through the next steps in finding Leo's killer, something the tea and cake hadn't helped with, although it had been lovely. Plus, it was fun to hang out with some friendly cats.

Maybe it was time for a career change. I could get used to looking after animals all day. Flipper also loved it.

I looked down and grinned at him. He had several cats following him around. He was in his element as he strutted along with his new friendly felines. If Jessie could see him now, she'd be jealous of all the attention he was getting.

I grabbed the newspapers and hurried over to Sandy.

"Thanks for doing that," Sandy said. "And whenever you want to start on the cat houses at your end, they also need their paper changing and fresh litter."

"I'll get right on it," I said.

"Any more news about what's happening to the sanctuary?" Sandy brushed her hands together and began to separate the newspapers out.

"You'll have a couple more weeks," I said. "Have you had any luck in finding a new job?"

"Nothing so far. I did speak to Julius about the possibility of getting involved with the animal park. It's not my ideal job, but I'll take it if I have to."

"He'll have to keep you on," I said. "You're great with animals. And there can't be that much difference between looking after a domestic cat and a lion."

"Apart from the size, killer claws, and wild desire to eat me alive, you mean?"

I laughed. "You'll be a top wild animal keeper in no time."

Sandy smiled at me. "I don't suppose you fancy giving up a life of paperwork and high tea with lords and ladies for a minimum wage job that involves all the free hairballs a woman can handle?"

"It's funny you should mention that. The thought had crossed my mind." I walked back along the cat houses to the boxes of newspapers. I grabbed my own handful and opened the first house.

One litter tray down and I was on to the next one. I shook out the cat litter and was just about to grab the dirty paper from the bottom when I noticed strange looking writing on it. It wasn't usual newspaper print. I dragged it out and shook off as much of the dirt as I could.

The air felt heavy and sweat broke out on my brow. I was looking at a copy of Leo's will.

The edges were soggy and stained, but I didn't care about that as I carried it out of the cat house and into the small office Sandy used.

I flattened out the paper. Despite the smudged ink, I could see that Leo had left almost everything to establish a charity so the cat sanctuary could remain on the estate forever. No wonder Lady Cordelia and anyone else who saw this will would want to keep it hidden. They were left with virtually nothing.

I continued to read the will, slowing as I saw a line about leaving money and assets to different individuals. There were small sums left for Julius, Tabitha, Montgomery, and Lady Cordelia, but it was the next line that was of most interest.

I hereby leave twenty percent of my remaining estate to Melinda Nell Babington.

Melinda Nell Babington? Nell was the first name of the cattery helper who'd been arrested for damaging Lady Cordelia's car. Did this relate to her? If so, how was she related to Leo? If they shared the same surname they must have a familial connection.

My heart caught in my throat. Could she be Leo's secret wife? Perhaps he'd married her without divorcing Lady Cordelia. That would explain why he needed to keep their connection a secret.

I looked up as the office door opened, and my mouth went dry. Nell stood in the doorway, her narrowed gaze on me.

"It looks like you've found something you shouldn't," Nell said.

"I thought you'd been arrested," I said, glancing around for a place to hide the will.

"I got released without charge." She closed the door behind her and leaned against it. "Lady Cordelia didn't see me damaging her car and the police weren't prepared to go with just her word that I was the culprit. It seems like money can't buy you everything."

I looked at the will and swallowed. "Do you know about this will?"

"I should, since my name is in it." Nell took a step toward me.

Now the door was shut, I caught a whiff of flowers. It must be Nell's perfume, the perfume Leo smelled just before he died. "I didn't know you and Leo were related."

"Nobody does," Nell said. "We're brother and sister."

So much for my secret marriage theory. "Why keep that a secret?"

"I'm his half-sister," Nell said. "Our mother had an affair and I was the result. She was sent away in shame to give birth to me and I was put up for adoption. It was a big scandal at the time, but the family was determined to keep it a secret."

"Leo found out about you?"

"I found out about him," Nell said. "It's hard to ignore a name like Babington. I came to the castle a few times as a visitor. It took me a while to believe I was supposed to be a part of this."

"You must have been angry that you missed out on so much," I said. "All the wealth and social status that comes with living here."

Nell shrugged. "The family who adopted me were decent enough, but I always knew I was meant for greater things. I never fitted in. In the end, they shoved me into a private school and I only saw my adoptive parents in the vacations. As soon as I could, I left home and spent a few years drifting around trying to find a purpose. I read about this place by chance in a magazine and started to do my own investigation." Her gaze settled on the will. "You can imagine how surprised I was when I found a reference to Lady Babington going away for a summer sabbatical just around the time I was born. I traced back the records and what do you know, I was a part of all this." She waved her arms around and laughed bitterly.

"Leo must have been thrilled when you told him you were his sister."

Nell smiled and some of the anger slid from her face. "He was. Leo was a decent man. He took me under his wing, gave me this job, and told me he'd figure out a way to make me a part of the family. I'd been here a year before I realized he didn't mean any of it. He was embarrassed about me."

"I'm sure he wasn't," I said.

"He never told any of his children about me," Nell said. "And he never told Lady Cordelia or Monty."

"Maybe he was just waiting for the right time."

"If it had been the other way around, I'd have introduced him to everyone without a second of hesitation. I'd have been so proud to have Leo as family. I'd have shown him off to everyone."

I looked carefully at Nell and saw how nervous she was, her hands shaky and her eyes darting around the office.

"And then Leo died," I said. "That must have hit you hard. You were only just getting to know each other."

"It probably hit him harder." Nell tittered and slapped a hand over her mouth. "I shouldn't say that."

I straightened my spine and took a deep breath. "I don't think Leo's death was an accident."

Nell's eyes narrowed. "What do you think happened to him?"

"Someone smothered him in his sleep."

"Have you asked Lady Cordelia about that? She didn't think much of her husband when he was alive."

"And what did you think about Leo?" I asked. "If he was embarrassed about introducing you to his family that must have been hard to take. Perhaps so hard that you decided to do something about it. He left you a lot of money in this will."

Nell snorted a laugh. "That will is pathetic. You should have seen the one he wrote before that."

"There's another will? What was in that one?"

"He left me everything," Nell said. "Well, almost everything. He decided his family had enough assets and they could do what they liked with the castle. Leo planned to set up a charity just for the animal sanctuary. He was going to let me run it, and was leaving me eighty percent of everything he owned. I'd have had enough to keep the sanctuary going forever. It was going to be his legacy."

I raised my eyebrows. "That was generous of him. What changed? Why did he write this new will instead?"

"He said he wasn't sure I could be relied upon. Something about me being unhealthily obsessed with the cats. I didn't have a clue what he was talking about. Leo loved them as much as I do. He was always hanging out here, talking to the cats and telling them his secrets. He seemed to think only he had the right to do that. I was the crazy one because I wanted to spend my time with four-legged friends rather than him. So, he made an amendment to the will. He still left me some money, but he didn't want me involved with this sanctuary. That wasn't right. I had to make sure that didn't happen."

"So you killed him."

Nell carried on as if I hadn't spoken. "Leo said he was going to set the sanctuary up as a charity and get a professional in to run it. I'm professional when it comes to the animals. I love them and always do what's best for them. He wouldn't listen to me. He kept telling me I should get help and needed to spend more time with people. Have a life outside of this."

I looked at the will again as the pieces clicked into place in my head. "After you killed Leo, you realized you had the rest of his family in your way. You needed to get rid of them before revealing your connection to Leo. That way, you'd get all the estate. Was that your plan?"

"People are harder to kill than I thought they'd be," Nell said. "I was sure I'd crushed Julius with that truck. When I looked out the cab window he was still waving his arms around and screaming. I was just about to reverse over him when I heard shouts from inside the castle and realized he'd been spotted. I only just managed to get away without being seen."

"And Tabitha? You messed with her car, didn't you?"

"I was certain I'd be able to get rid of Tabitha thanks to her terrible driving. I knew what cable to cut through, so it should have been easy to make her crash look accidental. She still survived."

"And Montgomery? What were you going to do with him?"

"I couldn't resist the opportunity to take him down when I spotted him lurking around the cat houses." Nell's eyes glazed over. "I was thinking of throwing him in the lake. I was going to do it as soon as I'd knocked him out. Then I heard footsteps and had to hide him and disappear before someone spotted me. I didn't think anyone would discover him in the maintenance room before I finished the job."

This woman was insane. "And Lady Cordelia? Was she also on your hit list?"

An evil smirk spread across Nell's face. "I had big plans for her, especially considering what she wants to do with our lovely cats."

I shuddered. "And Leo?"

"Poor Leo," Nell said. "I smothered him with a cat bed. The one he kept in his bedroom that the enormous ginger cat liked to sleep in. That poor cat got accused of all sorts of things after Leo died."

I recalled how Big Ginge reacted every time someone suggested he'd killed Leo in his sleep. No wonder he got angry. That poor pussycat was innocent.

"I felt bad I had to do that to Leo, but he wasn't listening to reason. Every time I confronted him about the changes he was making to his will he got angry." Her gaze flicked to the papers on the desk. "What you're got there is his most recent will. None of the family have seen it, other than Cordelia. They won't like it when they do. It means their money will be diverted to the cats."

"Lady Cordelia knows about you?"

"She had her suspicions, especially after she read that will and saw my name in there. Of course, I use a different surname in day-to-day life, so she couldn't prove anything right away. But I knew she was looking into my background and wanted me gone. That's why she sacked me and had me arrested for spray painting her car."

"You didn't do that?"

"She probably did it herself," Nell said. "She'd do anything to get rid of me. But believe me, the feeling is mutual."

"The family has a right to know what happened to Leo," I said.

"And I have a right to what's mine," Nell said. "And these cats have a right to live out the rest of their lives without worrying about being thrown away or abused like they've already been. Nobody should ever be abandoned. It's not fair."

The door behind Nell seemed like a long way away as she advanced toward me, her fingers reaching out to the will on the desk.

"I can't let you have this." I grabbed the will and clutched it to my chest, ignoring the scent of cat pee that drifted up my nose. "It's only fair that Leo gets justice for what happened to him."

"So long as these cats are well looked after, Leo won't care what happened to him." Nell held her hand out. "Give me that will. I thought putting it in a litter box was a fitting end to the copy I had. Then I got arrested before I was able to burn it. Now you've found it, which is a shame, because I get the impression you love animals."

I backed away from Nell. "I do. I love them. Nothing bad will happen to these cats while I'm working here."

"But you're not going to be working here for much longer," Nell said. "I need you out of the way so I can get rid of the family and claim what's mine. If you go telling the police or anyone else what you know, my plan will be ruined."

I continued to back away, and walked through an intense cold spot. My breath plumed out in front of me and I shuddered as Leo materialized by the desk.

"What's wrong with you?" Nell asked.

"I've just seen a ghost," I whispered, delighted by Leo's perfect timing.

"You'll soon be a ghost." Nell crouched and glared at me. "I'll take that will from you if I have to pry it from your cold dead fingers."

"I could do with some help here," I said to Leo. "Here's your killer."

Nell's eyebrows shot up and she glanced over her shoulder. "Who are you talking to?"

I licked my lips. "Leo."

Nell laughed, but her gaze shot around the office. "Leo's dead. I should know, I was there when he took his last breath."

Leo frowned at Nell and then looked at me.

"She did it," I said. "Nell didn't like the changes you made to your will. She wanted more of the family estate. She felt she was owed it after what happened to her."

"I was owed it," Nell said. "Stop talking to yourself and give me that will."

Leo shot through the air toward Nell and shoved her backward.

She staggered a few steps and frowned, before advancing toward me again.

Leo wrapped his arms around her and spun her toward the door.

Nell let out a yelp. "What's happening?"

"Leo's not happy with you," I said.

"But Leo's... dead."

"That doesn't mean he's at rest," I said. "How can he be after you killed him?"

"I only did it to get what I was entitled to," Nell said. She flung her arms in front of her face as Leo shoved her again, and staggered backward, landing in one of the big buckets of cat litter stored in the corner of the office.

Leo shoved the office door open and Flipper, Big Ginge, and the three cats who'd been following Flipper around, ran into the room and launched themselves at Nell.

She screamed and covered her face with her hands as Flipper landed on her chest and lay down. The cats circled her, hissing and nipping her hands and any exposed pieces of skin they could find.

"Get them off me!" Nell tried to push Flipper off her chest, but he bared his teeth and growled at her.

"I thought you loved animals," I said, relief running through me as Flipper and the cats did an amazing job of restraining Nell.

"I do!" Nell said. "But these ones are possessed. I don't know what's wrong with them. Animals always love me."

"They don't love you now," I said. "Not after what you did to Leo, and what you were trying to do to everybody else."

A whimpering moan came out of Nell. "I deserve that money."

I looked over at Leo and could see his ghost was already fading. "Are you happy?" I asked. "We found out who killed you. You can be at peace now. And the rest of your family are safe. I'll make sure the police know what happened and your new will is read."

Leo drifted toward me and pressed an icy kiss on my cheek before blinking out of sight.

I lifted the phone on the desk and dialed the police.

Chapter 22

"And as a thank you for what you did, apprehending that dreadful Nell, you may stay in your job if you wish." Lady Cordelia peered at me from the other side of her desk.

"And no more cat litter duties?" I asked.

She pressed her lips together. "No more litter duties unless you wish there to be. And the sanctuary is staying. It can be Leo's legacy. He clearly wanted the cats to remain here."

"And what about his new will?" I asked. It had been twenty-four hours since Nell had confessed to everything. Since then, I'd barely had a moment to myself as I'd explained everything to the police, updated the family, and made sure they all got to see what was in Leo's most recent will.

"That's a private family matter." Lady Cordelia leaned back in her chair and sighed. "But I will ensure his most recent requests are undertaken. I may not agree with his fascination with cats, but I see they were the biggest love of his life. He wanted to make sure they were well provided for. The relevant paperwork is with our solicitors and the matter will be taken in hand. The cats' futures are secured."

"That's all I wanted to hear," I said.

Lady Cordelia looked at the corner of her desk, where Big Ginge was fast asleep, curled in a patch of sunshine. She leaned over and stroked his head. "And I must admit, this one is beginning to grow on me. I just wish he wouldn't keep leaving his hairballs everywhere."

"Love cats, love hairballs." I stood and smiled at Lady Cordelia. "And since I did help figure out what happened to Leo, I don't suppose Helen and I can have the rest of the day off? We're house hunting, and need to go and look at a few places. I've been neglecting my own private life recently."

Lady Cordelia narrowed her eyes but then nodded. "Take the day off. I could do with some time off myself. Finding out that Leo was murdered and some crazy woman was trying to bump off the rest of us is enough to give everybody a shock. Let's start afresh tomorrow morning. You meet me here and we'll get to work on my admin."

I left the office with a smile on my face, giving Helen a thumbs-up as I spotted her on the stairs. She grinned at me and raced away.

I got the impression everything was going to be okay between me and Lady Cordelia from now on. We hadn't gotten off to the best of starts, but I'd shown her I was more than capable. And now Leo's ghost had gone, things would get back to normal.

As I walked out the front of the castle, I saw Sebastien standing by a waiting cab.

He raised his hand in greeting as he walked over to me. "I'm glad I've seen you. I was just been getting my final things together."

"It's all over with you and Lady Cordelia?"

"I promised you I'd finish things with her," he said.

"How did she take it?"

"Better than I thought she would," Sebastien said. "She was already angry with me for the way I'd spoken to Julius. He did exactly what I figured he'd do, and told her all about our fight. I refused to apologize and said I couldn't handle her spoiled children. I also said I wanted some freedom to go traveling. She hated that idea. We've agreed to remain friends."

"And did you take any money from her?"

"Not a penny," Sebastien said. "And before you ask, I didn't accept Julius's offer of money either."

"But you were tempted," I said.

"It was half a million!" Sebastien gave me a look of mock surprise. "Even you'd have been tempted by that amount."

I gave him a hug and we said our goodbyes just as Helen hurried out the front door, her car keys in hand.

"Come on, we're going to be late." She grabbed my elbow and led me to her car.

"I've never seen you so keen on house hunting." I slid into the passenger seat, and Flipper jumped into the back seat.

"Zach reckons this place is ideal," Helen said as we shot along the driveway and out onto the road. "It's only half an hour from here as well, so if you decide not to tell Lady Cordelia where she can stick her job, it'll be perfect for us."

"I'm keeping the job for now," I said. "I've come to an understanding with Lady Cordelia. I even think she's thawing on the issue of the cats."

"I knew she would," Helen said. "She's finally acknowledged how brilliant you are. And who doesn't love cats?"

"The sanctuary stays as do all the cats," I said. "And Sandy gets to keep her job as well."

"But not Nell," Helen said.

"No. She was in shock after being hassled by the animals," I said. "Plus the ghost attack by Leo. She was babbling to the police as they led her away about some spirit attacking her. She's not going to have anything to do with cats for a very long time."

"Serves her right," Helen said. "But what about Tabitha's gross cat fur addiction? They won't be safe from her if she's still around."

"Lady Cordelia was made aware of that nasty problem. Tabitha is being packed off on an extended retreat. I have a feeling it'll involve a lot of therapy."

"And the animal park?"

"On ice for now. I think it will happen in the future, though."

"Well, so long as the cats can stay and they're safe, that's the main thing," Helen said. "And of course, Leo isn't bothering you anymore."

"Leo's gone. He seemed happy now all his requests are out in the open and Nell's been caught."

"Excellent. Now, keep a look out for a sign for Beaumont Fields."

"Is that where the house is?" I asked.

"It's around that area." Helen grinned as she guided the car around a corner.

I looked at her suspiciously. "Is there something you're not telling me?"

"Just you wait," she said. "I think you're going to love it."

Fifteen minutes later, we pulled up behind Zach's Land Rover. Zach and Gunner were both leaning against it when we arrived.

Zach walked over and gave me a kiss as I got out of the car.

"So, where is this wonderful house?" I looked around the country lane we'd stopped on and only spotted a couple of tiny cottages, a village shop, and a pub.

"I thought we'd go for a drink first," Zach said.

"And it sounds like you need one," Gunner said. "I've been hearing all about your exploits in your new job. You caught a killer."

"It's not so unusual." I grinned at Helen. "What about the house? We don't want anyone else to snap it up if it's as good as you think it is."

"Nobody is going to steal this house from us." Zach took hold of my hand and led me over the road into a thatched pub called the Drapers Arms.

We ordered our drinks and sat around a table. From the smiles on Zach and Gunner's faces, I could tell they were in on the same secret that Helen was keeping from me.

"What's going on?" I asked.

"Zach had an idea," Gunner said. He pulled a roll of paper out of his jacket and spread it across the table. It was an architect's drawing of a house.

"Since we've been having so much trouble finding our own home," Zach said, "I figured we may as well build our own. We all know what we want, but we can't find it in one building."

"Creating it ourselves is the only answer," Gunner said.

Zach looked over at me. "What do you think?"

I stared at the plan, looking at the spacious bedrooms, massive downstairs living area and lots of outside space. "It looks amazing."

Zach took hold of my hand and smiled. "We can have it just how we want it. And there'll be absolutely no risk of any unwanted visitors."

"Unless we do something silly, like build it on a graveyard," Helen said.

Gunner glanced at Zach. "I'm not sure what you both mean by that."

"He means the ghosts, idiot," Helen said.

Gunner's eyebrows shot up. "Oh, yes. The ghosts. It all makes sense now."

Helen tutted at Gunner, and he grinned at her.

"Where are we going to build our dream home?" I asked Zach.

"There's a plot of land just down the road from here that's for sale," Helen said.

My mouth fell open. "How much do you know about this?"

"I've only known for the last couple of days," Helen said. "Zach and Gunner made me promise to keep it a secret from you because they wanted to tell you themselves."

"I hope you don't mind," Zach said. "I swore Helen to secrecy because I wanted to show you the plans first. We can finish these drinks and go and look at the land. I'm sure you're going to love it. There's loads of space for the dogs, amazing views, and it'll all be ours."

I looked at the plans again and a big smile crossed my face. This was the perfect solution. We could all get what we wanted. I wouldn't be bothered by restless ghosts lurking around in an old house, and we could take our time creating our ideal home.

I raised my glass. "This calls for a toast."

"To a ghost-free home," Zach said.

Gunner opened his mouth, but Helen frowned at him and he shut it just as quickly.

I shook my head. "To a home where everybody is happy."

"To having the biggest bedroom and an attached bathroom," Helen said.

"To having space for all my vinyl and a place to play the drums whenever I like," Gunner said.

Helen frowned. "You play the drums?"

"I'm in a band, baby," Gunner said. "Do you think musicians are sexy?"

Helen's cheeks flushed and she looked at Gunner with wide eyes.

I laughed as we clinked our glasses together. I grinned at everybody around the table. This was going to be paradise. Noisy, messy, sometimes difficult paradise, but I'd happily take it.

***

Want to find out how Lorna's paradise plays out? Get Ghostly Rules and meet the new ghosts in Lorna's life.

Read on to learn more.

Dark deeds. Missing gold. A ghost with twenty-five million secrets!

Lorna Shadow, Helen, and Flipper arrive at their new jobs to find a family in mourning and a ghost with an attitude. Will there ever be a job she gets that doesn't involve a ghost?

When Lorna discovers the family is full of 'reformed' criminals, she must watch her step as she figures out who killed Lonnie Cornell and where he hid the stolen gold. With a new house to pay for, Lorna can't afford to lose this job, but will the stubborn ghost, eerie feelings she keeps experiencing, and menacing suspects be too much to handle?

She needs to be careful with her sleuthing or she'll wind up on the hit list of some seriously scary people.

Never one to run from a challenge, Lorna questions mobsters, wives with secrets, and family members who are on the wrong side of shady to get to the truth. It'll take more than tea and cake to get Lorna through this twisty mystery.

Complete series list

Ghostly Manners
Ghostly Secrets
Ghostly Games
Ghostly Affairs
Ghostly Business
Ghostly Rules
Ghostly Waves
Ghostly Play
Ghostly Proposal
Ghostly Vows
Ghostly Fright
Ghostly Hunt
Ghostly Surprises

About the Author

K.E. O'Connor (Karen) is the author of the adorably fun Lorna Shadow cozy ghost mystery series, the wickedly funny Crypt Witch paranormal mystery series, the Magical Misfits Mysteries featuring a sassy cat with a bundle of twisty puzzles to solve, the slightly darker Witch Haven paranormal mystery series featuring four troubled witches and their wonderful furry (feathered and web-slinging companions), and the whimsical, delicious Holly Holmes cozy culinary mysteries.

Stay in touch with the fun mysteries:

Newsletter:
www.subscribepage.com/cozymysteries
Website:
www.keoconnor.com
Facebook:
www.facebook.com/keoconnorauthor